IN THE
CASTLE
OF THE BEAR

IN THE CASTLE OF THE BEAR

by Steve Senn

ATHENEUM 1985 NEW YORK

Library of Congress Cataloging in Publication Data

Senn, Steve.
In the castle of the bear.

SUMMARY: Jason hates everything about his new life after
his father remarries especially his stepmother, whose
efforts to be a firm parent drive them further and further
apart, until a grave crisis reveals a common bond and a
possibility of friendship.
[1. Stepmothers—Fiction.   2. Suicide—Fiction.
3. Family problems—Fiction.   4. Interpersonal relations—
Fiction]   I. Title.
PZ7.S47In   1985   [Fic]   85-7951
ISBN 0-689-31167-2

Published simultaneously in Canada by
Collier Macmillan Canada, Inc.
Composition by Yankee Typesetters, Concord, New Hampshire
Printed and bound by Fairfield Graphics, Fairfield, Pennsylvania
Designed by Judith Lerner
First Edition

IN THE
CASTLE
OF THE BEAR

1

JASON Barnett watched from a balcony as the
church filled up with flowers. People spoke in
hushed tones and went about like mice below.
He fidgeted in his suit; the collar was too tight, and
the knot of his tie pressed into his throat. And he
was hot. The sun of August lit up each bearded
saint, each trumpeting angel in the windows like a
pattern of fire. The air bled with their color.

He hated the color and the light. Funerals should
be in rain. The sky should be a blanket of total
lead, with not even lightning for punctuation, and
the rain should drizzle.

It had rained at Mother's funeral. Only a little,

but the sky was dark all day, with clotted clouds. He had only been ten then, but he remembered it clearly. And then last year, when he was eleven, the collie Pablo had run in front of a truck. A mound had flowered in the back yard for Pablo. Daddy had dug it in the rain.

A funeral should be black. But the clothes today would be sparkling white, the organ music bouncy and glad. He had seen some of the relatives already, excited and wearing pink lacy dresses. This was another kind of funeral for Jason Barnett. Today his father would marry again. It was like burying his mother a second time.

There was a sort of trapdoor in the big stained glass window over the balcony, and he could look out over the arriving cars and the treetops of the small southern town. It was near enough to the town where they lived so that everyone would be coming.

He tried not to think about the new woman, whose town this was. He did not want her to come live in their house. He did not want to mix memories. It was a mystery to him why Daddy was marrying her, anyway. She was big and fat and blonde. She wasn't pretty.

The organ music was beginning. The pipes went up the wall by the balcony, and they throbbed with power. It was starting. It made him want to throw open the door of the belfry beside him and swing on the ropes until the bells rang like crazy. And when all the people had gathered, he would tell them that a woman had bewitched his father, and it was all a terrible, terrible mistake.

Suddenly, the door opened. He gasped and jumped back. It was *her.*

"There you are. We couldn't find you."

She was all white, like a cloud of lace, with tiny white flowers in her hair. She filled the doorway. Her hand was stretched out to him. He realized in disgust that she almost looked pretty.

"Come on, Jason," she insisted. "You're an usher. You know you have to help out down here." She smiled. "I thought you might be brooding up here. Let's go!"

She found his hands and led him down the stairs, past the great silent bells with their still ropes. He did not resist.

Jason waited in the stuffy darkness of the car while all the happy people spilled out of the church. His tie was off, in his pocket where it couldn't hurt him any more. And from that pocket he had taken the stub of a pencil and a piece of paper. Using his leg to bear down on, he had written three or four lines stacked beneath each other. But he couldn't concentrate on the poem—there was too much happening.

This was Tilton, the new bride, Lauren's, town. It seemed very difficult to write a poem here, the way he always could at home when he needed to get stuff out of him.

Tilton was also the regional headquarters for the tractor company his father worked for. Daddy had always spent a lot of time on the road, selling, but about a year ago he had begun coming to Tilton even on the Sundays he didn't work.

Sometimes he took Jason with him and dropped him off at the zoo. There was nowhere else in that part of the state where Jason could see elephants and anteaters and bears. Then, one day when Daddy picked him up at the place next to the bear house where he always waited, *she* was in the car. Daddy seemed in an especially good mood. She drove back with them that day, to stay with friends and to meet Dad's relatives. They explained to him they were getting married. And she tried to make jokes with him and be chummy. But they had ruined everything for him, and he was icy. To make matters worse, his sisters liked her. They *would*. They talked together about dresses and cooking and things. And Jason had gradually begun to feel less like a part of the family and more like an exile.

Suddenly there was somebody scrabbling at the car door. Before he could hide his half-finished poem, the door opened and a girl in a pink dress slid onto the seat beside him. She was sixteen, four years older than Jason, and she was laughing.

"Look, the usher's writing another poem," she giggled to the girl who climbed in after her, who was only a year younger. "Is it to your girl friend?"

Jason stuffed the paper into his pocket and glared at them. They were the Foreign Princesses, his sisters.

"You didn't even have any cake, silly," the closest one, Jill, said. "It was as big as you are."

"I bet *she* ate half of it," he said.

"Oh, knock it off," the younger one, Tracy, said. "Lauren's not that big. I don't think she even had any cake."

"I think she was too excited." Jill laughed. "She almost couldn't say 'I do.' "

"You did just fine, though, brother," Tracy said, patting him on the knee. "Didn't fall down, or nothin'."

He pulled his leg away. "Wish I had."

Jill craned to watch the church doors. "*I* wish

Aunt Ruth would hurry up. I've got to go to the bathroom."

"I wish we could go with them on their honeymoon," Tracy said, then giggled when Jill gave her a dirty look. "Well, I've never been to Jekyll Island! And they could have a separate room."

Jill frowned. "If we went, it would be like being in the same room even if we stayed in different hotels. People need to be by themselves on their honeymoon."

"Rot," Jason muttered. "I sure am glad we didn't have to go."

Tracy eyed him. "You could stay home anyway. And I want you to stop that nasty talk about Lauren. I like her. She's an artist."

Jason made a face. "Yeah, but nobody's ever seen any of her old oil paintings except Daddy. She's just an insurance clerk."

"Come ooonnnnnn, Aunt Ruth," Jill chanted.

"I just don't like the idea of her living in our house," Jason said. It was not her place. It was Mother's place.

"Do you think we should tell him, Jill?" Tracy said out of one corner of her mouth.

"What? Oh, that. We'd better wait for Daddy to tell him."

"Tell me *what?*" he demanded.

"Can't tell." Tracy now pretended cool.

He grew furious. "Tell me WHAT?"

"Oh, for Heaven's sake!" Jill snapped.

"That Lauren's *not* going to live in our house," Tracy blurted out. She let him grow truly perplexed, then explained, "We're going to go live in *her* house. Here, in Tilton."

"We're not," he responded angrily.

"Yes, we are," Jill confirmed. "And I'm finally getting a bedroom away from this twerp."

"*Twerp!*" Tracy shrilled.

"But what about my room? And the magnolia tree?" Jason cried in anguish.

"Here comes Aunt Ruth. Hallelujah!"

But Jason was no longer listening. He was looking over the trees, in the direction of Lauren's house. Everyone had known but him. Even the Foreign Princesses. Each Princess would have her own room now and would grow even more foreign. But worse, it was *her* territory. What would happen to his poems now? She was luring them all to the place where her power was strongest. And Daddy would be away most of the time, so it wouldn't matter to him. Only Jason understood that something bad was coming, and there was no way he could warn them.

He clutched the pencil and paper tightly in his pocket, as though they could somehow protect him, and tried to smile at Aunt Ruth.

2

ON SATURDAY after the honeymoon they drove the giant rental van loaded with all their furniture from home to Tilton and moved much of it in the same night. Jason had a blurred image of stacked boxes in long brown halls, flowered carpets and alien smells. They managed to get into bed only a little before midnight.

He was awakened early the next morning by bells. All the churches of Tilton were calling. The Barnetts were too exhausted to get up and dress for church, but Jason was glad of the bells' call. It gave him a chance to take stock of his new surroundings. He went to the window in the hall outside his room. It was on the third floor, and he could see everything from it.

The house sat on a hill among pecan trees, over-looking the town. The big old place had probably watched the town grow from just a few houses at a crossroad, had probably seen secret things, things that it would never tell. Three stories of dark wood, it seemed stitched together with staircases. And from one corner of the house there rose a tur-ret, a round tower with a shingled peak, and a win-dow that surveyed the town shyly, through the fingers of the trees. It was a house of an earlier time.

He explored it before anyone was awake. The house's insides were a dark maze, with intricate aged furniture, faded oriental rugs, and thick dust that made sunbeams into spangled ghosts. Jason could imagine Edgar Allen Poe living there and writing his poems. At first it seemed like the man-sion in "The Fall of the House of Usher." But then it reminded him more of a castle, dark and drear. And from that moment that was its name.

It was the Castle.

That first day was spent arranging furniture and sweeping the disturbed dust of the old place around.

All the clothes had to be sorted out and misplaced boxes found. The Princesses were at each other's throats by the end of the afternoon, and Jason was enjoying the fight until Lauren appeared. Her presence in the doorway stilled all their words. She spoke in crisp, stern tones that sent them to their rooms and a chill jolt up Jason's spine. The Princesses didn't argue the way they did with Daddy. There was something dark and powerful in Lauren's eyes.

Monday was a free day, and there was a whole week before school started. A whole week of freedom before he had to face more newness. He played around the yard of the Castle, discovering hidden niches and strange caves of shrubbery. Then, in the afternoon, Lauren allowed him to explore the town.

It was all familiar, because it was the same sort of little town that he had come from, and yet it was new. New stores, new alleys, new old ladies to scowl at him from new old porches. Tilton had a courthouse of red brick, tall and with a clock high in its tower. And a bronze statue on the courthouse lawn. The Baptist Church in Tilton, the one where the wedding had been, was older than the one they had gone to before. It had a high steeple and fancy stone scrollwork around the windows. It looked down at him as if it remembered who he was.

It took hours to walk around Tilton, from the Castle to the edge of town where the dusty peanut mill sprawled. He was at the mill watching lines of peanut trucks unload when a tremendous sound pierced the other noises. He spun to see a great steam whistle blowing high over the mill buildings. It was the six o'clock quitting whistle.

He had not noticed the sky reddening toward sunset behind the town, and he hurried his footsteps back toward the Castle. He felt good. It was not a bad town, after all. Maybe he would write a poem about it after supper.

But he slowed his step as he neared the Castle, and he paused before opening the front door. Once inside, he understood why. Lauren stood in his way as if she knew just when he would appear. Her hair was tied up with a scarf, and she was dirty from unpacking things. She wore a cold, tight expression that made Jason look down and try to go around her, and everywhere there was a zoo smell, the odor of frightened animals.

"What time is it, Jason?"

Her tone stopped him. He looked at the big grandfather clock by the stairs. "Six twenty."

"And what time did I tell you to be back here by?"

His heart seemed to plunge down an elevator. He had forgotten she had put a time limit on his travels. "Six o'clock," he said finally.

Then she just looked at him. Her eye was pale and cold, and he had the awful feeling that he had committed some kind of crime.

"Go on," she said. "Wash your hands. Supper's waiting on you."

When he got to the table, everyone was there already, and he realized they had been waiting for him. Tracy looked at him with obvious pleasure at his discomfort.

"Jason," Daddy said, "I understand that you told Lauren you would be back here by six."

"But, I don't have a watch!"

His father looked bewildered, as though he hadn't thought of that.

"It doesn't matter," Lauren said calmly. "You know when the sun gets low that it's near six."

"The point is," Daddy continued quickly, "I want you to try to start doing what you tell us you're going to do." He looked at Lauren and then put his hand over hers. "This is something I haven't been too good at since . . . for the last couple of years. I've been lenient. I've told Lauren all about this, and she wants to help us all get back on track. So now that we've got a complete home again, you're expected to be home on time."

Jason felt cheated, betrayed. On trial. "But, I was only a few minutes late!"

"Late is late," Lauren said softly, but as firmly as stone. "We're not going to do anything this time, but the next time you come in after six you will miss supper."

Jason had other things to say, but he knew that they would do no good. She had already gotten to Daddy. She had probably cornered him a minute after six and made him agree to all this. It was so unfair! Jason took a bowl of peas from Tracy without looking at her. He could feel her gloating gaze on his face, and he wouldn't give her the satisfaction of looking up. He ate, but woodenly and in silence, and he hoped Daddy saw how miserable he was.

After supper he went up to his room and shut the door. He cried loudly into his pillow. But no one came to see what was wrong. When he did hear footsteps, it turned out to be the Foreign Princesses going to their rooms. They stopped outside his room, and he softened his crying to listen.

Tracy said something in a sympathetic, pitying tone.

"Oh, Tracy! He only does that to get someone to baby him. Leave him alone."

He couldn't make out what Tracy said to that. "Honestly, Daddy never makes him do anything. I think it's a good thing he's finally going to have to grow up."

Then the girls' voices trailed off as they continued to their rooms. Jill's words left a spike of ice in his heart. He forgot entirely to cry.

An hour later he went downstairs and watched TV with the family. Nobody seemed to notice he was there. No one semed to care at all.

That night he dreamed of the Bear.

He was in a car, which someone had parked and left him in to wait. At first he seemed to be in a garage, but then he slowly began to realize that it was a cave. It was very black. This did not bother him at first, but slowly the blackness came closer to him. It poured into his eyes like a liquid. It was warm, and it seemed to know things. Then he heard a noise. He was glad, because he thought whoever had left him was returning, but gradually he realized it was something else. Something was snuffling and sniffing and scratching at the far end of the cave. He knew it was a bear, and he was filled with terror.

3

S CHOOL started the next week.
He welcomed it as a refuge—Lauren was not there. Each new day had become a wilderness, thicker and more overgrown with rules. Rules that he forgot. Rules that he could not understand. Rules about *everything*.

His gladness lasted until he got to the classroom. When he saw Mrs. Quarterman, he began to realize this might be as bad as the Castle. She had a thin, pinched face with glasses, and a chin that was pushed into her neck. Her eyes were like needles. The other kids in his class were a blur of new faces, and the faces that didn't look scared looked frightening.

There were tests. Jason did all right on the English one and on the spelling quiz. But then Mrs. Quarterman handed out the math test. It was mostly fifth grade problems, division and multiplication. Jason felt a mild surge of fear. He would have failed math last year, but Mrs. Lee had liked his poetry and helped him a lot.

Mrs. Quarterman patroled up and down the aisles during the test. Jason was always aware of her. And the smell of purple ink choked him as he tried to remember how to do long division. He erased and erased as he forgot what numbers to carry over. When she called time, he was barely finished with half the problems, but at least the test was over.

The math test ruined lunch for him. But in the afternoon there was P.E., and he felt free for a time. He wandered around, watching the different groups of kids form and drift into games. Some kids asked him to join in a baseball game, but he said no. He didn't like to be on teams. Instead, he watched from a safe distance, mildly interested.

Gradually he became aware of another kid on the hard-packed red dirt beside the baseball field, one who was not a part of the game but was not watching it either. He was a tall, wiry kid, drawing in the dirt with one sneakered foot. Jason tried to ignore him, but was soon watching in fascination. Circles. Big circles were what he was drawing. And now he was writing carefully around the circles. Jason casually edged over toward him.

The kid noticed him approaching and tried to pretend he was only doodling in the sand. Jason said nothing, but examined the figure on the ground.

"Agla . . ." he read aloud. "Bethor . . . Lilith. What does that mean?" He eyed the kid curiously.

The kid grinned sheepishly and shrugged. "Oh, I was just fooling around. Doesn't mean anything."

Jason looked at him intensely, then back at the ground. "And what are those squiggly things in the middle there? Is that a star?" He read more of the strange words. "Elion . . . Tetragram . . ."

"Don't say it!" the kid gulped. Jason hadn't finished the word, which was *Tetragrammaton*.

Jason slowly grinned. "It's magic, isn't it?"

For the first time the kid looked back at him. He paused, then nodded. "Sort of. How'd you know?"

"It's a magic circle. I read about them. But where did you find out how to draw one?" Jason felt a rush of excitement.

The kid shrugged again and looked hard at him. "I won't tell. I swear."

A small smile grew on the kid's face. "I found it

in some books in my aunt's house. At least it used to be my aunt's house. My cousin Tilda lives there now. There's a big box in her attic, with all these old books in it. Some of them got rotted covers, they're so old. Part of that circle was in a book. I made up the rest, so it's not real magic. I mean, you couldn't really call up anything with it."

Jason nodded sagely. He would do anything to see those books.

"You know much about magic?" the kid asked. He took a wandering step closer.

"Just a little bit. Mostly about the kind they had when knights were around. Wizards and alchemists."

"Alchemists?"

"The guys who used to live in castles and try to turn lead into gold for kings. It's kind of like magic, with potions and mixtures."

"Oh. Yeah. This is different. Have you ever read any H.P. Lovecraft?"

"No." Jason felt a surge of jealousy rise and fall.

"He talks about this kind of magic. You have to stand in the middle of the circle when you're calling up spirits. It protects you from them."

A memory flickered in Jason. "And you're supposed to use a wand of hazelwood, too, aren't you? That's what warlocks used."

The kid looked at him with obvious respect. "You know what warlocks are! You're probably the only other kid in Tilton that knows that."

Jason shrugged, feeling embarrassed. "We just moved here."

"Whose room are you in?"

"Mrs. Quarterman's."

The kid made a face. "Quasimodo! Boy, I sure am glad I didn't get her."

Jason laughed at Mrs. Quarterman's new name, then felt a sinking feeling and remembered the smell of purple ink. "Yeah, she's a witch if there ever was one. I think she put a spell on my math paper already."

The kid laughed, and Jason saw that one of his teeth was chipped. "Math is easy. It's spelling I can't do."

"I wish we could trade subjects. At least you can look up words in the dictionary to see how to spell them."

"Not if you can't spell them in the first place."

They both laughed. But then, like midnight chiming to break a spell, the bell rang, signaling an end to the play period. The kid quickly kicked sand over the magic circle. Jason helped, before the baseball players could see it. Jason understood. These things had to be kept from ordinary people.

"What's your name?" he asked as they joined the flow of students. "Mine's Jason Barnett."

"Cleve Adams. Meet you after school. We can talk some more."

Everything seemed to go better once he had met Cleve. They walked home together every day, and Jason's envy of Cleve's knowledge grew. But his excitement grew faster, and the envy never had a chance to fester because Cleve always explained the secrets to Jason.

And for nearly a week, Jason managed to stay out of Lauren's way. Daddy was away on one of his trips, but Jason was used to that. Lauren had an eagle eye out for him, but by a minor miracle he managed to remember all the rules. On Tuesday and Wednesday nights after supper he excused himself to do his homework. But that was saved for last. First, he examined the books that Cleve had smuggled from his cousin's house and given to him. They were scholarly and hard to read. When he tired of them, he would turn to his big book of Poe's stories and poems and pretend that it was he who pondered over "many a quaint and curious volume of forgotten lore."

Then came Thursday, and he turned in a division paper that he knew was done all wrong. Mrs. Quarterman took him aside and explained all the steps carefully, as if he were hard of hearing, or stupid. Jason said he understood, but knew he was lying. After that a feeling of sadness came over him that not even Cleve could shake.

He tried to make a poem about it, but the right words hid from him. That night he had dreams he didn't even want to remember. Darkness, caves, and the Bear.

4

JASON dried the last supper dish and quickly slid it into place in the drain. Lauren had assigned him the dishes on non-school nights, and this was Friday. He smiled, for he had finished in record time.

He set another record getting to his room. He slipped the secret book he had to return to Cleve tonight into his pants and covered the top part of it with his shirt.

But before he could get to the front door Lauren caught him. She stood in the kitchen doorway, and the light threw her shadow all the way across the foyer floor.

"Wait a minute, Jason. I want you to see something."

Fuming, he followed her back into the kitchen, where she began taking the dishes out of the drain and examining them.

"You don't have to be in such a big hurry," she said quietly, not looking at him. "You've got all weekend to play. Where were you going?"

"Over to Cleve's." Jason shrugged. "I told Jill."

Lauren's gray eyes flickered up to meet his. "You tell *me*, not your sister. I'm the one responsible for you."

He held her gaze defiantly, but said nothing.

"Look at this," Lauren said, pointing at a streak on the underside of a plate. "What's that?"

It was banana pudding. A tiny trace of it. Jason still said nothing.

"I want you to do these dishes again, and do them right this time. You have eyes. I don't want to see this kind of carelessness with the dishes again. Okay?"

Jason nodded, tight-lipped. They stood there for a minute, and he had the impression there was something more she wanted to say to him. But he wouldn't look up. He wouldn't give her the opening, and he turned away when she tried to put her hand on his shoulder. She left quietly, and he was alone with the dishes.

After he had finished, he refused to go to Cleve's. Everything was spoiled. He went upstairs and read until Jill called him downstairs to the phone.

It was Cleve. The phone was in an alcove near the living room, so he had to whisper, especially since what Cleve had to suggest was a secret. The conversation was short.

Later, after everyone else had gone to bed, Jason was still awake. He was writing poems by candlelight, the way he imagined Edgar Allen Poe did. He was fully dressed, and he looked at the clock repeatedly. Finally, near midnight, Jason put his pen down. The poem went in the file folder he kept secretly taped to the back of his desk. It was time.

It took only a few moments to sneak into the tower and open the window. Another moment, and he had climbed into the pecan tree and from there to the ground. He stealthily made his way down the hill to Orange Street, where the oleander bushes would hide him. Cleve was waiting there.

"Did you have any trouble?" he asked anxiously.

"No. They're all sound asleep. Especially her. I think she snores."

They began walking down Orange Street. There were few lighted windows this late at night. Only rarely did a car pass them. Once in a while a dog barked a warning not to enter some territory or other and, if they didn't, slowly quieted again. They were alone with the darkness. It was a privacy both cherished in this tight little town.

The air was close and warm, and the crickets loud. Jason felt he could breathe again. "Ah. I'm free."

"My parents are bad," Cleve sighed, "but I'm glad I don't have a stepmother like yours."

"I think she really is a witch."

Cleve shrugged. "Probably not. I don't think adults know how mean they seem to us sometimes."

"She knows," Jason said firmly.

"Maybe not. Maybe she feels as strange as you do about your moving into the Castle and all. She probably wants your dad to think she's really being a good strong mother to you is all."

Jason looked down a side street and turned that way. "Did you read that poem?"

" 'The Bells'? Yeah. I kind of liked it. I didn't know Poe wrote things like that. It was strange."

Jason looked at Cleve sharply. "It's my favorite poem. 'The bells, bells, bells, bells, To the moaning and the groaning of the bells.' "

It was Cleve's turn to change the subject. He brought up the approaching Halloween, not as a party time, but in the old meaning of a sacred festival to appease the ghosts. Cleve told how the Castle used to be considered a haunted house, when Lauren's old aunt lived there; and on Halloween kids would run up on a dare to ring the doorbell. Now that new people were living there, it would probably become a legitimate place to trick or treat. Halloween led them to talk about vampires and vampire movies. The night grew older, and a succession of street lamps welcomed them over and over into false dawns between the cool spaces of night.

"I don't really think Dracula could turn into a bat at all," Cleve commented after a long period of silence in which they only walked.

"Why? I thought all vampires could."

"That may be just what the peasants thought. The bats might be a vampire's familiars, that's all."

"What do you mean?"

"Familiars. You know, like a witch's black cat. All black magicians have an animal to go and do their bidding. Really it's a demon, but it takes the shape of some animal. It goes and spies on the victims, or drives them toward their master. That kind of stuff."

"And maybe the bat was Dracula's familiar?"

"Yeah."

"What about werewolves," Jason pondered. "I wonder if they really change into wolves, or just send a familiar that's a wolf."

Cleve looked astounded. "I never thought about that. But I hope it's not true. I like the idea of Lon Chaney slowly getting hair all over his face and growing claws."

"You said there was a book in your cousin's attic that had werewolves in it, didn't you? See if it says anything about familiars."

"I don't know," Cleve said. "Tilda said I've been spending too much time up there. The only time I can do it is after school, and she's writing then. She writes stories and tries to sell them." Cleve brightened. "Hey, maybe you could show her your poems sometime and see what she thinks."

Jason didn't answer. He hadn't told Cleve that his poems were very, very secret. But he vowed never to show him any more. Or any more of his favorite poems by other people, either. If Cleve knew anything at all about poems, he wouldn't suggest Jason show them to a stranger.

"Familiars are really scary," Cleve said, trying to restart the conversation. "Sometimes a warlock can send his familiar into your dreams, to chase you. Warlocks can drive people crazy that way."

Something flickered across Jason's mind. Something dark. "Can a familiar be any kind of animal?"

"I guess. But usually it's something that's like the warlock's personality. I guess it could be anything."

They had reached the limit of Tilton's street-

lamps, and they swung around by the yellow secu-
rity lights of the peanut mill and headed back. The
conversation drifted from witches to talk about
wars and knights and tournaments.

They were tired, and it was very late, and in his
enthusiasm for talking, Jason forgot all about familiars. Or thought he had.

5

THE ANCIENT, decaying garage behind the Castle had always been locked before. But this Sunday afternoon, Jason noticed from across the yard, a door was ajar.

It was a big building, past its prime fifty years ago. It leaned, and its wood was weather-gray. Jason had heard that it used to be a coach house, when the Castle was new and there were few automobiles. Its great door swung open easily.

Inside, the floor was dirt. Shapeless, collapsed antiques huddled around the walls. Magazines from decades past lay in molding stacks everywhere. Stillness had been living here alone for a long time.

Jason took a faltering step, wondering what ghosts might object to his entry. But, also, he wondered what books might lurk here. Maybe there were treasures like the ones in Cleve's secret attic. Volumes of forgotten lore.

Magazines crumbled into sodden flakes as he probed. Spiders ran from the antique paper avalanche, but their webs whispered across his face and clung in haunting strands. The spaces between boards in the walls were wide, and bars of bright sun splayed over the gray wilderness, but he could find no books.

But then, behind a wall of rotten record albums, a bar of light fell across a child. It was only a painting of a child, but it gave him a start. It was dusty, and the kid was dressed in flowing white lace from long ago. It was a nice picture. Behind it was another one; this one he pulled out of the mildewed stack. It was a knight in armor. The paint curled in glints on his helmet. It was neat. Maybe he could clean it up and take it to his room . . .

Then he saw the name scrawled in the corner in thick white strokes. Lauren Lee. It was one of *her* paintings.

The garage grew brighter, and he thought the sun had come out from behind a cloud. Then he realized the door had swung further open, and he spun.

Lauren stepped in without seeing him and let the door clack shut behind her. The canvas clattered from his hands, and she flinched, nearly dropping the jar of turpentine she was carrying.

"Jason! You startled me. What are you doing?"

"I—I was just looking around. I wasn't doing anything."

She put fingertips to her chest and sighed. "Whew. I thought you were a ghost." Her eyes darted to the canvas on the floor. "Oh," she said in a softer voice, "I see you've found the archives. That's a lot of the stuff I did when I was young. You like Sir Lancelot there?"

"It's okay," Jason muttered.

"You can have it if you want to. As a . . ."

"No. No, it's okay. I was just snooping." He hurriedly shuffled the painting back in its place.

She seemed embarrassed that he had found her pictures. She smiled. "I wish I could still paint like that. You don't have as many hang-ups when you're young. Say—maybe I could get a little of that freshness back if I painted someone young. Would you mind sitting for me?"

"You mean, paint a picture of me?" Jason was terrified. He shook his head vigorously. Suddenly he wanted very much to get out of there.

"Well, think about it. Maybe you'll want to later. Maybe we could do it for Father's Day."

He mumbled something vaguely agreeable.

"Your father would like that. You know, he's told me about how good you are with words. I'm glad to have someone else creative around. Maybe we could . . ."

"I—I've got to go now."

He wheeled and stumbled out into the light. Then he ran. Away from the dark, choking garage. Away from her. He wasn't like her, and he wouldn't let her think that he was. He would never help her with her stupid old paintings.

Rarely did the Foreign Princesses get home from school before five. Either they stayed at friends' homes and did homework, or hung around the Burger King talking with boys. And Lauren worked at the accountants' office until around six.

Jason had the Castle to himself for an hour or two after school. And today, he gloried in it. He sat in the living room, in an overstuffed chair, and wrote a poem at a marble-topped table. It was a stormy poem, and it rhymed, so he had to gaze off into space and search his mind for the right words. He was Kipling. He was Poe.

"Let her wonder about me," he muttered to himself between stanzas. "She'll never find out about my poems." That would be like giving away the deepest secrets about himself. No one must know.

The right word finally came, and his pen raced across the page. That line led to another, and the meaning of the poem veered so that he had to concentrate to keep in control. It was then that he began feeling more than alone in the house.

The silence took on a new dimension; concentrating became impossible. The quiet no longer seemed passive. The spaces in the house were listening to him. A tickle of alarm fluttered across the back of his neck.

Something was watching him.

He did not turn fast enough to see what he felt in the doorway behind him. It was now merely a black space. But he had *felt* . . .

Think of something else, he told himself. Don't let the old Castle trick you into believing in things not there. Concentrate on the poem. What rhymes with "sword"? There was nothing in the doorway.

He had almost decided on "lord" when something moved down in the Castle's entrails. A definite noise. He swallowed heavily and put down his pen. He had heard it. What did it sound like? A person on a stair? A cabinet shutting? Something brushing against . . .

A creak, a groan. Or a partial rattle, muffled in the maze of rooms.

He was standing now, listening. The silence was so loud it was sound itself, calling him. But he knew the direction from which the noise had come. The basement. Lauren's lair, where she went to paint. Maybe she had stayed home today.

Or maybe it was only a draft in the old house, the wind having its joke. There was no reason for something to have been spying on him anyway. He took a step, two, toward the basement door. His hand groped around the dark corner, feeling across the bricks for the light switch, dreading to meet cold fingers waiting for his. But the light came on, revealing blank steps down to the concrete. Nothing was there. But there was still the laundry room, around the corner.

Under his breath he recited "Gunga Din." The rhythm of the words gave him strength. But they couldn't hide the awful creaking and groaning of the stairs. It sounded a lot like what he had heard before. Something could have been standing on the stair, looking at him from the darkness.

He did not have to finish reciting the poem. There was nothing in the laundry room out of the ordinary.

It was only a draft, then. Just wind playing in

the arcane spaces of the house. Then Jason remembered a movie he had seen, one with an old house and noises that turned out to be made by a draft inside a secret passage. You had to turn a candlestick, and part of the fireplace rolled back to reveal a doorway.

Of course. A secret passage. All old houses had them. That must be what the noise was.

That, or some invisible spirit traveling through the house. But there was no reason for it to have been examining him. All he was doing was . . .

Writing a poem. The very thing Lauren wanted to know about.

His eyes danced to the door to Lauren's studio. Did she keep it locked? Could something have dashed in there to hide when he turned on the lights? There, at the bottom of the door, around the crack . . . was it hair? *Hair?* All gray and wispy and matted as if some big animal had squeezed past. No, no, it was just long filaments of dust. It had to be that, didn't it?

But he did not want to try the door. It might not be locked. Suddenly he did not want to think about any of it anymore. Why had he come down here?

Upstairs, the front door slammed shut. Jason shivered. Tracy was home.

6

IN A FEW days Jason had nearly forgotten his suspicions. Then, one night after supper he found his old *Dracula* movie poster folded away in a suitcase and decided to hang it up. He was using his shoe to pound in the tacks when he noticed that a place on the wall in the corner of his room sounded different from other places: flat and hollow. He rapped again. Again the echo rang thinner, emptier, than it should have.

There were no clues to the change in sound in his room. The wall was blank. He slipped into the hall and paced off the distance to where his room must end. There, despite the dim light, he found a seam in the wall. Square, about the size of an oven door. It had been painted over many times. It lay in a shadowy zone beyond the reach of both hall lights, so it had been easy to miss all this time.

A shiver ran in zigzag safari up his back. "A secret passage," he whispered to himself. "I knew there was one someplace."

With his pocketknife he searched around the seam for a weak place. He found one. While chipping away paint, he noticed that the door had once had a handle on it. Strange, for a *secret* passage.

There was a lot of noise downstairs, but he wasn't listening. There was always noise in this cavernous house. Now he was so occupied that he didn't realize the noise was coming closer, up the tower stairs, angrily.

"Ja-*son!*"

It seemed to him Lauren had just materialized in the hallway. He dropped the knife as he scrambled up, heart pounding, to face her.

"What's tonight, Jason?"

"W-what do you mean?"

Her lips disappeared in rings of pursed muscles. He had to come up with the answer she was looking for fast.

"Oh. It's Thursday." Fear floated high in his

throat. Thursday he was supposed to take the trash out. He hadn't.

"Yes. Thursday. Why didn't you answer me when I called?"

He knew why. Because he had been intent on discovery. "I didn't hear you."

"Jason, the whole house heard me. The people in the graveyard heard me." She sighed, and all her impatience seemed to flow out of her. "If you expect to get your allowance, you're going to have to remember the trash. I can't hunt you down every Thursday and Sunday night."

"Okay," he mumbled, hoping it was convincing. Meanwhile he covered the pocketknife with his foot.

"Not okay." Her hands were on her hips and her eyes were narrow. He knew the signs of hassles-to-come by now. "I mean it. If you don't start remembering your chores and getting the dishes clean, I'm going to ground you."

Jason didn't reply. There was no use in talking. Sometimes when she made him feel like this, he didn't think he would ever talk again. They stood in the hall like magnets repelling each other, and he could feel her searching through her mind for more words. But his silence gave her no opening. Finally she solemnly asked if he understood her, and he nodded mutely. She headed back downstairs, and Jason followed as soon as he had snatched up his knife.

The outside air was nippy. His breath frosted as he lugged the trash cans out to the road. Then, the last can spilled. He had been going too quickly to get a lousy job over with, but it wasn't his fault. He filled with sudden fury at Lauren.

"She's trying to get me," he muttered on the way back to the house. "She wants to know about my poetry. She really didn't call, either. She wanted to make me feel guilty. She just snuck up on me. She can't wait for me to screw up. I hate her just as much as she hates me. One day I'll . . ."

In the bright kitchen doorway a great dark shape was reared, listening to him. Terror overwhelmed him. The listener was so silent and huge.

Lauren's voice said, "If you have something to say to me, say it where I can hear."

He didn't know what to do. She had heard every embarrassing word. But she moved aside to let him pass. Inside, she cornered him in the kitchen. How could she catch him *every time?* It was as if she followed him secretly to steal his thoughts. Or sent a spy. He didn't want to, but he had to face her.

For a long moment she just looked at him.

"Let's get something straight. I don't like having

to ride you like this any more than you do. You haven't had a lot of discipline, and it's rough getting started. I'm not going to let you do nothing, the way you're used to. I want you to start growing up."

Jason glowered. His face was turned down, but his eyes were on her. He wouldn't give her any words.

"All right. But listen to this." Her finger shot toward him. "We have to live together whether you like it or not. Your father and I are married. That makes me responsible for you. You can cooperate, or you can fight me. But things are going to happen my way in this house, no matter what."

In this house. Suddenly he knew how locked up he really was. This was her place. He was hers now. But he didn't answer.

There didn't seem anything else to say. He was at the door of the kitchen when he heard her say something else. He turned. Her back was to him.

"It's a dumbwaiter, I said. The thing you found in the hall."

Jason's jaw went slack.

"Or it used to be a dumbwaiter. A kind of elevator. They moved up food from the old kitchen in it. A hundred years ago." She began putting dishes away, slowly. "My aunt said they used it some when she was a little girl. But not for a long time. I wouldn't try to open it up, if I were you. It could be . . . dangerous." She glanced at him, and her eyes wore a strange, defeated look.

He reeled. She knew everything. As he returned through the blackness of the house, he realized she had seen the knife, knew what he had been doing every moment. It was as if some silent, invisible guardian traveled inside the Castle walls to whisper all Jason's secrets.

Jason turned the corner of Walnut Street to find a figure ahead of him. It walked in the canopy of shadows thrown by overhanging dogwoods. His breath frosted like fog in the chilly air and further obscured the figure. In a few steps he realized that it had stopped. It was waiting ahead.

He tried to convince his footsteps of their bravery. But nothing could make him forget Lauren's invisible guardian, or dread a meeting in the dark with . . .

He slowed.

"Jason?"

Cleve. He relaxed, and his steps quickened. "I knew it was you," he said.

"Where are you going?"

Jason shrugged. "Just wanted to get out of the Castle. She really hates me tonight. She can find out whatever I'm doing in that house. It's spooky."

Cleve glanced at him closely. "You think she has the Knowledge?"

Jason's voice went steely. "I *know* she has." He wanted to say more, but he had no proof.

They began walking, side by side through the dappled shadows.

"I'm going over to Tilda's," Cleve said. He seemed cautious tonight and kept glancing at Jason.

Jason ignored it. "Do you know what a dumbwaiter is? I found one in the hall outside my room. I thought it was a secret passage at first."

Cleve knew about dumbwaiters. He explained it better than Lauren had. The dumbwaiter went through a shaft in the house, from the lower kitchen to each floor. That way they could send food up to a sick guest's bedroom without climbing stairs. A few of the old houses in Tilton had them. They worked with ropes and pulleys.

Jason had been cool to Cleve since the last time they had walked, when Cleve had said those things about his poetry. But now it was good to talk again. The streets fluttered by.

Suddenly Jason realized they were standing in

front of Cleve's cousin's house. A light was on in the First Baptist Church next door, and a stained glass window bled into the night.

"Do you want to meet my cousin?" Cleve said after a long, awkward pause. "I think it'd be okay. But she's funny. If she's in one of her moods, we might have to go. She's like that. That's why my mom sends me over to eat breakfast with her every morning . . . she needs the company. Want to go in?"

Jason shrugged. What he really wanted to do was keep walking with Cleve, but he would go inside with him. That was second best.

Tilda, a thin woman with a small, beautiful smile, opened the front door. Her smile faltered only a moment when she saw Jason. She let them inside, into another century, where walls were covered with small, framed pictures and rugs were ornate prairies. Somehow the buttery light seemed cast by lanterns instead of electricity. Tilda had inherited her house, too, from an aunt, but it was more as if the house had inherited her.

She served them tea in delicate, elderly cups.

"How do you like living in the old Lee place?" she asked Jason. "It's one of the very oldest houses in Tilton."

"It's neat. It has a dumbwaiter."

"Oh. I remember them. I stayed in a house in Baltimore that had two."

"I don't know if this one works or not." Jason glanced up at the intricate wallpaper of the dining room. "How old is this house?"

"Not too old," she said. "Fifty or sixty years. Your house is over a hundred." Then, as if her dark eyes read his mind, she said, "This place looks so old because my aunt Flora moved everything here from her parents' house and tried to keep things the same way they had. It's hard to keep things the way they were when you were young. I guess she succeeded, though. And I haven't had the courage to change anything." She sent a long glance through the brooding rooms. "It takes a lot of courage to change things."

"I heard you've got a lot of old books," Jason said. Cleve tried to kick him under the table, but missed. Jason grinned.

Tilda smiled. "I thought boys were only interested in getting away from books."

"Not old books. Full of forgotten lore."

Tilda laughed. She looked at their eager faces and sighed. "But don't forget that that kind of thing can make you weak and weary." After a pause she said, "I suppose I'd be cruel if I didn't take you on a tour of the attic, then."

"You don't have to," Cleve protested.

"It's all right. It's been so hard for me to get any work done anyway . . ." She cleared the teacups away without finishing her statement.

After lighting a single candle, Tilda led them up a folding stair through a black square of an opening. The air was close, as if they breathed the darkness. Shadows lurked beyond the weak light's reach, over and behind stacks of boxes and chairs and antique oddments. They bumped along a dim trail between things. Jason's heart surged. This was like true Poe. Tilda's pale dress flowed around her like a shroud. And her skin in the candlelight was a beautiful pearl color framed by long dark hair. Their clumsy sounds came back at odd angles from unseen sepulchral walls.

"Here it is."

The trunk was huge. It creaked with age, and its inside was musty as a tomb. But instead of bodies lay ranks and stacks of books, which breathed the life of forgotten ages when he opened them.

"Here are the ones I was telling you about," Cleve whispered, warming now to Jason's enthusiasm.

Ancient History, Curious Myths of the Middle Ages, Witness of Darkness, Jason read. *Alchemy, The Cult of Asmodeus, The Hammer of Witches.*

The trunk was an open doorway; and scanning the brown pages by candlelight, Jason felt as if he had broken into some Pharaoh's crypt.

Too soon Tilda seemed anxious to leave. She appeared to have drawn more into herself as the boys hissed and squealed in discovery. Her shoulders, which before had been delicate, seemed bony and braced against an invisible weight.

And then they were all back in the normal, conscious part of the house. No candles. No secrets. Jason had wanted to borrow half the books he had seen. But somehow it had not seemed possible to ask. If he asked, he felt, all the books might vanish.

He and Cleve whispered fiercely about the titles while Tilda wandered into a room with a fireplace and began poking at the embers. Aimlessly, they followed her in. She shivered, though it did not seem cold to Jason.

"Seeing old books always depresses me," she said to no one. For some reason Jason followed her gaze to a desk top. There lay stacks of papers covered in handwriting. She noticed his look and smiled wanly. "Old books remind me of other people's accomplishments. And how they faded."

She slid the papers in a drawer. It was an embarrassed motion. She did not want them looking at what she was writing. Jason understood.

The mood had changed. Cleve tried to brighten things up again.

"Jason writes poetry, Tilda."

Jason shot him a fiery glance. His secret, his precious and closely watched secret, had been violated. But Tilda was looking at him.

"Do you?" she asked softly.

He nodded, then shrugged.

"Would you bring me some, sometime? I'd like to read them."

"Okay," he said without warmth. He would never let someone actually read his poems.

He looked up. Tilda was staring at him. And for a moment he did not feel so stupid, or different. It was like seeing a familiar kingdom through the fog.

7

THOUGH the year was well into fall, the days were still bright, and that Sunday was one of the brightest. He still carried the excitement of meeting Tilda bound and stuffed inside the Sunday suit with him. With the sun so bright, and his recent pleasure, he felt as if it were summer. That must have been what did it, he later decided—he was made giddy by excitement and sunlight.

For halfway through the sermon, during the gray part that made even adults nod off, he began writing on the back of his program. Half in a dream, he imagined things in the scenes of colored light around the walls, as he used to do in church. A poem started to grow. He never remembered what it was about. Maybe summer and green things. Something happy, for when Mother nudged his knee, he took it playfully and nudged back. She was always doing things to tease him when he was trying to concentrate. He wrote on and had to stifle a laugh when she nudged again . . .

Then, of course, he realized where he was and who was sitting beside him. He looked up. The window behind Lauren glared so brightly all he could make out was her shape, and one eye in the mist of her face, looking at him. A poem was there, naked on his knee, and she reached for it.

No! He had been stupid, stupid to drift off and let her see into his secret land. But he would never let her come further! She held a corner of the paper and looked over his shoulder to read it, slipping her arm around him like an octopus. He grabbed the poem, crumpling it. His hand ate the paper until all that was left was the corner she held.

"Jason!" she whispered close to his ear. "What are you doing? I just want to see the program!"

He wouldn't let go. When she gave up, he balled the paper into his pocket and kept his hand there to guard it.

Lauren continued questioning him, but all he

told her was that it was nothing; it was just his paper.

But he knew he had done something fatal. He had let her bewitch him into thinking she was Mother and had let her know his deepest secret, his poetry; not even Mother had known that.

He found a way through the panel in the hall.

But inside there was only a shaft that went down forever. His flashlight did not show the bottom. Some ropes hung down. They moved through ancient pulleys in the shaft's roof, but barely. A dumbwaiter.

Jason knew there had to be another secret passage, if this was just a dumbwaiter. There had to be a great, dark secret within the Castle walls. And now that she had glimpsed his secret, he had to find hers. That would be a way of getting secret power over Lauren.

Besides, if there was no secret passage, that meant there was something moving about in the Castle unseen. Something that he did not understand, but that he dreaded.

He found the attic, a cavern as dark as a bat's dream. But inside there was no treasure like Tilda's. Just old boxes and curtains. And time—layers of it lying in a sleep over everything.

His attention turned to the tower that ran up one side of the Castle. It ended in a silvery cone, like a witch's hat, like the roofs of towers on story-book castles. But that was only from the outside. From the inside, the tower ended in a flat ceiling. Yet there had to be a space inside the cone. Something had to be up there.

So one afternoon he took a flashlight and searched the tower ceiling, piling up boxes until a chair would reach it. The ceiling was divided into squares, and he tested the grooves with his knife. He had to be careful. The chair teetered, and below was the deep staircase. His arms ached from holding them overhead. But there was no panel. No room in the tower peak.

"It must be somewhere else," he whispered to himself.

To climb down from the chair he had to juggle his weight, and that was tricky. At the last minute he toppled and had to make a grab for the light fixture in the ceiling to steady himself. It wobbled, and he glanced up.

"There it is!" he said excitedly. "I knew it!"

The carved glass bowl that fitted over the light bulb turned. It was a latch, and four squares in the ceiling formed a door. It swung up into blackness.

There he paused. Whatever he searched for

might be up there. And it might know his secrets, too. It might be Lauren's spy. Perhaps it had lured him here.

He recited a poem under his breath for courage and climbed up inside the tower room. It was cold, and the aroused dust choked him into a coughing fit. There was nothing there, though, once he focused his eyes to the dimness. A blank bell and empty floor. The dust lay like snow, like ashes. His light searched the floorboards for sign of a hidden handle or hinge, but there was . . .

There was a pattern. Four or five smudges in the dust, following each other oddly, right across the floor. It was almost as if they were . . . footsteps. But they couldn't be. They went directly across the floor, from wall to curving wall. As though something had passed through, and the floor had only accidentally interfered.

Suddenly, cold slithered across his back. He shivered.

"A familiar," he said.

What shape was in the prints? Tremblingly, he examined the nearest one. Was it a cat? No . . . too big. And the stride was too great. Something had been here. Some horrible thing Lauren had sent to haunt . . .

And then he remembered the dreams, and the

creature in them. The smell of the zoo. Lauren's shape reared in a lighted doorway.

What shape were the footprints of a bear?

He spent the rest of the afternoon, until the Princesses got home, in the living room cuddled against the fading daylight. Once home, they teased him about his explorations of the Castle and made strange, veiled comments about Lauren. After a little of their abuse, he felt better about going into the upper part of the house. His room felt safer with someone else in the place.

What he'd found in the tower room scared him. He had only half believed in the things he and Cleve had talked of before. This was like being a Dracula fan and then finding a coffin in your basement. It was too real. Jason felt feverish, and he wished he'd never gone looking for the secret passage. Knowing was worse than suspecting. Familiars were real, and there was one in this house.

If only that had been the worst thing he learned that day.

When he came downstairs for supper, there was something strange in the air. Everyone but him seemed to know about it. Daddy was home. He was beaming as if he had been gone for a month instead of four days. His hug was tighter than usual, the odor of after-shave distinct.

Lauren busied herself with the roast, which had been cooking at low heat all day while she was at work. She was flushed and paid more attention to what she was doing than she had to. It was as if she were about to go on stage.

Jason began to realize they were having a feast. A roast, on Monday? With three vegetables and rolls? Still, it was a good supper; Jason started enjoying it. And the Princesses were funny for a change. He wasn't in all their jokes.

Daddy seemed to be waiting for a special moment. His eyes sparkled. But Jason could not make contact with him. Mostly, his father looked at Lauren. And Lauren said little. She did not even comment on his table manners, but kept her eyes down.

Something was coming. He had found out about the Bear. Now Lauren would have to do something about his discovery. Jason could feel it in his stomach muscles.

Suddenly Daddy interrupted the girls and raised his glass. "I'd like to propose a toast to my talented wife," he said, beaming. Everyone but Jason drank. No one noticed that he didn't.

"Lauren is beginning a new career, starting in a week," he continued. Dread began growing in Jason. "She's not going to be an insurance accountant any longer. I never thought she should be. You've all heard me talk about her painting. But I don't think any of you know that's how I first met her. At the Carroll County Art Show. Well, she's going to be an artist again. But not just on Sundays. Every day. Right here in our house."

Jason came unanchored from the floor. He felt his heart swing up, captured by the thing that even now might be roaming upstairs.

"She's going to take up painting full time. And I'm going to sell her work. I'll take the pictures with me when I'm on the road. There are a lot of art galleries between here and Atlanta."

Lauren looked shyly down at her plate and smiled. But Daddy forced her to look at him, and she grinned.

"What do you think about that?" Daddy punched him lightly on the shoulder. But he didn't feel it.

Jason wasn't there. He was a thousand leagues off, in a dungeon. Just when he was beginning to discover things, she was putting a stop to it. He had found out too much. She would be home to make sure he didn't find out more about her secrets. And she had fooled everybody else into believing she was staying home to paint.

Later, as Jason did the dishes, because the Foreign Princesses were too busy, Lauren found an excuse to bumble about in the kitchen. She put things away and tidied up, but Jason stonily ignored her. Her triumph was complete enough without giving her the satisfaction of his attention. At last he felt her standing beside him. She wasn't doing anything, so he had to notice her.

"I just wanted to tell you," she said softly, "that I hope my being at home won't disturb you too much. I don't expect I'll be upstairs when you get home, anyway."

As if that made any difference. He listened.

"I'll mostly be down in the cellar. That's where all my paints are. . . . Anyway, I just wanted to tell you that painting is just one of the reasons I wanted to quit work."

Now she's going to say it. His jaw muscles tensed.

"I never liked leaving you alone. I feel like a kid needs to have someone around . . . just in case. It's not good for you to be all alone in this big old place."

Sure, he thought. Sure. Make it sound like you're doing me a favor.

"Anyway, I know we haven't hit it off right. Maybe I've been too hard. But now, I hope we can make peace, since I'll be around in case you need help with your homework or something. Or even if you get lonesome. So come see me. Watch me paint. We can talk."

Jason nodded. Once. If only she wouldn't pretend to be nice to him, he thought. Then he wouldn't hate her so much.

She picked up one of the dishes he had finished. "You're really getting a lot better at washing, Jason. Remember when you first came here? Boy, were you bad."

Lauren grew bubbly. "I just know things are going to get better around here now that I'll be home. I feel like I've been freed from some kind of bondage. I feel as if I could fly."

She flies—I'm chained up, he thought. But after a few more minutes with no response from him, she drifted off into the other room. Good.

In the night, something called to him.

He did not know what it was, but it wakened him into jagged alertness. Suddenly, from a dreamless sleep. He sat up in bed and listened. The night filled his ears. Had it been a sound? Had it been his name, aloud. Did it come from the hall?

Through the cracked door he could see all the way to the tower stair. The darkness there was alive with possibility. Then he noticed the shadow. It moved slowly against the pane of the hall window, and he could not see what threw it. It was just a dark spot in the pattern of moonlight. He could not remember if there was anything outside the window that would normally cast a shadow. It was a roundish, moving shape. In a moment it drifted out of the frame of the window.

All his courage helped him get to the hall. But there was nothing on the ledge outside the window, to his relief. Nothing in the yard but a pine tree. Nothing in the sky but a pale quarter moon. But something had come between the moonlight and the window. Something, perhaps, had come to look in on him. Maybe something that wanted him to know it was there.

On the window there was a fading patch of fog. A moment before, something warm had been there, outside. Breathing?

Suddenly, terror gripped him. It had been there, drifting like a cloud outside the Castle. The Bear. The spirit-bear she had made for him. It was loose. It wanted him to know—that's why it had wakened him. It was no longer just watching him and reporting back to Lauren. Now that Jason knew her secret—that she was a witch, that she had a familiar—the Bear meant to keep him from learning more.

It was a warning.

8

"BUT, DID you actually *see* it?" Cleve asked. "No. I mean, not face to face. It doesn't want me to see it yet. It was just a warning."

"Wow, this is *strange*," Cleve said as they walked. He was trying to swallow Jason's story of sorcery and haunting. He nearly had. After all, they both believed in such things. Didn't they?

Jason picked up the pace, which had slackened as he told his story. He wanted to get home with plenty of time before the Foreign Princesses, so he could show his evidence.

"But it was there," Jason said. "I think I heard it again just before sunrise. I'm not sure."

"But what is it warning you about?"

"To stop. It doesn't want me looking for its secret passages."

"But you didn't find any."

Jason ignored him. "I must have been close to something. Why else would she quit work? It's to keep an eye on me. There's a secret to her power, and she knows I can find it."

The Castle came into view, and they ran the rest of the way up the hill. It was musty and dark inside, but it was familiar to Jason, and he relished seeing how impressed Cleve was with it. They went to Jason's room, where schoolbooks were safely deposited. Then to the hall window. Cleve studied the view thoughtfully.

"You don't think it could be here now, do you?" he asked, gazing around him at the dark Victorian spaces.

"Probably not. Most likely it only comes out at night, when she can concentrate."

Cleve nodded. "It really takes a lot of energy to make a familiar. I know that."

They examined the window ledge for telltale scratches, but the paint was unblemished. Then, as they bent in scrutiny, there was a sound from deep somewhere in the house. Cleve jumped.

"It's just the furnace," Jason said, smiling.

Then, a moment later as they discussed how big the creature was, a hot breath rippled across their backs. Cleve squealed in fear, and Jason almost fell. They ran, and only when they collided at the tower stair did they realize nothing was after them. Back at the window, Cleve pointed to a grill in the ceiling.

"It's the vent. It's blowing hot air."

They laughed in relief, both happy that the other one had been fooled too.

"Wait a minute," Cleve said suddenly. "The fog on the window last night: could that have been from the vent? Did you notice if it was on the inside of the glass?"

Jason shook his head. "It was on the outside. It was shaped like breath."

Cleve looked at the window, then out into the yard.

"Anyway, I saw the footprints in the tower room! C'mon."

In a few minutes Jason was turning the light fixture to open the trapdoor. It swung into blackness.

"There," he said, and clambered up into the opening with the flashlight in his teeth. Cleve came up after him.

The light wallowed around the curving walls and came to rest on the dust-thick floor. It took a moment of search for Jason to find the right set of smudges.

"See? They go across this way."

"Let me see the light," Cleve said, reaching.

"Why?"

Cleve took it and shone it around. They looked for a long time at the gray expanse of the floor. It was like the moon—dusty, pocked, mysterious.

"Look, the footsteps go this way. Right across the floor, headed over there. There's one. And there are four more, see? It's kind of dancing, kind of wobbling as it goes. It wanted me to know it had been here, all right."

"But wouldn't a bear make deeper marks?"

"It's not an *ordinary* bear," Jason said, putting an edge in his voice. "You know that. Gravity doesn't affect it. How else could it walk through walls and float up to high windows?" What was wrong with Cleve? *He* knew about the supernatural.

Cleve examined the marks again, for a long time. His light beam traveled slowly over all of the floor. "Do those really look like bear tracks to you?" he finally said.

"Sure. They couldn't be anything else."

"What about those?" He pointed the light to other depressions in the dust. Squarish ones.

Jason shrugged. What was all this questioning about, anyway? He shot a sharp glance at Cleve.

"It looks as if somebody was storing boxes up here, to me," his friend finally said. "Look. Those could be human footprints. See? They go right across to that square shape, as if somebody was picking up a box . . . I can't tell about the prints." He shook his head. "I can't."

Jason followed him out of the tower, silently.

"What about the shadow at the window?" he said, tight-lipped. "The light was coming from the moon, overhead. Whatever was there wasn't throwing a shadow from below. It was at the level of the window."

It was Cleve's turn to shrug. "You could be right."

"But what?" Jason could feel the doubt. It was cold.

Cleve looked at him and glanced away. "It could have been something from the yard, if a car's headlights threw the shadow. The trees, maybe."

Jason didn't say anything. There wasn't any point. He silently picked up Cleve's books, started downstairs, and soon heard Cleve following. They did not exchange words until Jason opened the front door for him, and then it was Cleve who spoke.

"What's the matter? I said you were probably right. I wasn't there, anyway. Those prints just didn't look like a bear made them, to me."

"I'll see you later," was all Jason said. He handed Cleve his books.

"What *is* it with you?" Cleve said sharply. "Have I got to agree with everything you say? Can't *I* think?"

Since there was no response from Jason, Cleve turned his back and left the house. In a moment, he was gone.

A friend would have understood, Jason thought, turning back into the Castle alone. Cleve wasn't the sort of person he had thought. He had seen the Bear. He had.

Only later that afternoon, before the Princesses came home, did he realize it was the Bear's doing. It had gone back to the tower and disguised its prints. And it had carefully hovered where the vent was, so that that could be explained away, too. It wanted him to be mad at Cleve.

It wanted him alone. *She* wanted him alone.

Jason began following Cleve to school each morning, always from a distance so that he would not know. If the Bear wouldn't let them be friends, at least he could stay in touch. At least he could do that.

Ghostlike, he paced Cleve's journey to school each day, and when the two met up at the school grounds he only nodded. Cleve ate breakfast at Tilda's house every morning, and Jason waited in the bushes at the First Baptist Church. It was a short breakfast, one of Cleve's duties, and she always came out to see him off. Pale and small, she waved.

He began wondering about Tilda more than ever. She reminded him of Lenore, in Poe's poems—the rare and radiant maiden. She wrote things, like Jason. And she didn't want people to see them, again like Jason. In the pool of life that was Tilton, she stood out. Cleve's mother—everybody's mother—worked. But Tilda stayed at home and performed mysteries in the parlor.

And Lauren was now coming home, to perform her own mysteries in mockery of his and Tilda's art.

He did not know he was going to end up at Tilda's house when he went walking one night. But he did. He went a different way than he usually did. It was a surprise when he recognized the house. He saw the church steeple beyond. Then he realized where he was.

Her study light was on. It made a neat yellow

square of the window, and Jason could see her seated at her desk. He looked down the street nervously. It was dark and deserted. He quietly crept up and looked in the window.

She wrote with the kind of pen you have to keep dipping in ink. He liked that. Page after page went onto the stack. Then she would look into space, and he could see her lips moving as though trying out words. Sometimes, she would get up and pace. Her hands would flutter in space, and she would mumble, working something out. Acting to herself whatever it was she wanted to make happen on the paper.

Watching her through the window gave him the same kind of feeling her eyes had. He felt less alone, even though he was outside the house, outside her world. It was as though they shared something without knowing it, and he had found out. Maybe, he thought, maybe he *could* show her his poems, sometime. Maybe she would know how to treat them.

She seemed to reach a snag. Putting down her pen, she read what she had written over and over again, then put her head in her hands for a long time. Finally she tore up the paper and threw it away from her, her face twisted in anger.

Jason drew away from the window instinctively.

He understood how she felt. He could get that angry at himself sometimes. That was why she had hidden her papers that day. It was not easy to do things as well as you wanted to.

Then an idea hit him. Maybe he could go up and knock on the door. Now. Maybe it would be good to talk to Tilda. He could tell her he understood about the writing. Then, maybe, he could tell her about the Bear. She would believe. After all, the attic books were hers; she knew about familiars and things. Together, maybe he and Tilda could fight the Bear.

It was a long walk to the front porch, and he used up almost all his courage making it. Once there, he found he could not touch the door. Something made him afraid. More afraid, even, than he had been when he discovered the Bear. Doubt covered him. He was on the verge of giving away all his secrets. What if she just laughed at him. What if she was on the Bear's side?

From inside the house came the muffled ringing of a telephone. He heard Tilda's footsteps traveling across the house. The moment was gone.

He carefully crept off the porch and continued his walk. There were lots of reasons why he shouldn't talk to Tilda, anyway. Not tonight, at least. Still, he could not shake a feeling of horror, a feeling that something good was plunging away from him. He nearly ran the last mile to the Castle.

That night the Bear filled the Castle, as though it was as big as a house. He dreamed of it, and when he awakened in the blackness, he heard it scratching through the winding halls. Ice shot all through him. He found that the only thing that helped was reciting poems. And he had to fight to hold them to a whisper. He wanted to shout out their protection.

The Bear had never been this strong before. Something was happening.

9

THERE was a mist the next morning, and a narrow coldness close to the ground. Wet leaves all over. Late October was playing at being winter. He could not tell what was happening in Tilda's house. He crouched slightly in the bushes beside the First Baptist Church and searched the features of the house. The fog blurred its shape just a fraction, making all the old Victorian gingerbread on the gables look like lace.

He began to wonder. Cleve had never stayed in the house this long before. He began to wonder if he should not go on to school. The house certainly did not look any different than it had those other times. Not until the police car pulled up to the curb, and hard official shoes crunched up the walk. Then, even though he crouched lower in the shrubbery, the house began to look sharper. It took on a new cast. It reminded him of the Castle, and he knew something bad was inside it. He was afraid. But he couldn't run now. They would see him. There were a million eyes in the house, all pressed to cracks in the blinds.

He was still, frozen to the spot, when Cleve's mother came speeding into the driveway. She left, pale-faced, with Cleve. He saw Cleve's shoulders shaking and heard the horrible sound of his friend's crying. Even after they were gone, the sound hung there. He couldn't move.

The ambulance people came, and now there was a clot of neighbors at a polite distance from the house. Mostly housewives in bathrobes. Their voices were low, but curious. Then the men brought out the stretcher, with the long, still bundle on it. They said something to the waiting women, who put their hands to their mouths and whispered among themselves quickly.

The policemen came out of the house and sent the women home with firm, evasive words. They looked around the outside of the house for a while, but they did not seem suspicious the way you would think detectives would be. They stood talking.

He turned to stone when he understood.

"Always was an odd one. Writing, and all."

"I guess that's what all those ashes were, in the fireplace. The stuff she wrote, I mean. Guess she didn't want folks poking through it when she was gone."

"Yeah. They'll talk enough as it is. Suicide's always like that."

"Good-looking woman, too. Shame."

"Yeah. Damned shame, ain't it?"

Then they were gone. The sun was up higher in the sky now, but he felt a lot colder. He came out of the bushes. The house was even clearer now.

What had made Tilda do it? He no longer cared if anybody saw him. He crossed the lawn and went to the window where he had watched her the night before. He could only see a narrow angle of the room, and nothing there looked sinister. No blood or toppled teacups.

Then he looked down. He had almost stepped on it. With a growing feeling of both horror and understanding, he realized why Cleve's cousin had gone. It was after her, too. It had come here to haunt her and look in her windows and torture her too.

Fog filled the mark in the soft dirt of the flower-bed. The policemen hadn't even noticed it. Nobody would believe him even if he told. He quickly kicked dirt into the footprint and tamped it down. They would just say it was the mark of a big stray dog. A big birddog or a shepherd. But he recognized the clawed foot, though it was disguised.

The Bear had taken its first victim.

10

HE CAME home each day, as before, but the Castle was different. It did not have that waiting animal atmosphere inside it. The air was warm, and the awful sweet smell of turpentine seeped up from the basement, where *she* now lurked every day. Lauren's presence was in the empty, mazelike upstairs, too. Jason took care not to make noises or talk to himself, because that presence knew he was there and was listening. The painting was just an excuse to keep her close to him.

He was no longer free to search the house or shout out the stanzas of his favorite poems to drive out the Bear. She had ruined the last activity that still brought him joy, now that he could no longer talk to Cleve.

He was trapped in the Castle, with her.

The first weeks she stayed home Jason thought he would go insane. The days were November-gray, and his mood was black. His math papers were exercises in failure, and tests were endless nightmares. Soon, Daddy would know what an idiot he was. The Bear was winning.

This must have been how it had been with Tilda, all routes of escape blocked, all hopes snuffed in that house beside the church. The Bear pressing down on her mind the way it now did on his.

All he seemed able to do was stare out the windows at the cold, sunless sky and feel dreadfully alone. Then the Princesses would come home, or Lauren would come out of her den and try to find excuses to talk to him, and he would have to hide in his room.

And the Bear was laughing at him, from some dark corner of the Castle. He could feel it.

It angered him that he could not fight back. And it was the anger, finally, that broke him free from the mood. It was a Friday. He stood frozen before the gray scene of sleepy Tilton, cursing the elusive Bear. He used up all the poems he knew and then made up some. *Kill the Bear, Kill the Bear,* became the chorus. Then, before he knew it, he was running. He felt as if he had a spear or an axe in his hands, and he had been sent by the king to rid the Castle of its ogre. Balconies fluttered past, and he raced around furniture wildly, pursuing the beast.

He stopped running when darkness loomed ahead and he became confused. He put out his hand and touched a cold stone wall. It dripped dank sweat, and it trembled. He was at the top of the basement stairs. The furnace was roaring below, condensing moisture on the wall.

Why had he come here? There was only Lauren here, in her secret chamber.

He didn't understand exactly why, but he crept down, holding onto the wall to keep his balance in the dark. By the time he reached the floor, he could see by the faint light leaking from under the door.

A radio played classical music, and there were occasional noises that he could not identify. He pressed his eye to the wide, rusty keyhole. He could see a table and part of an elbow that moved occasionally, but nothing else. Nothing that made him feel better.

Suddenly he had a burning, itching desire to know what she was doing in there. Exactly what was she painting? Was she really alone? Could *it* be in there?

If he could just see her and figure out why she did things the way she did, it would be as good as tracking the Bear. Then he remembered the dumbwaiter, and how it went through the upper floors to the basement.

He raced breathlessly upstairs, stopping long enough in the kitchen to search for the big oil can before hurrying on. Two more flights of stairs rushed by, then he was in the high hall beside the turret. He pried the cabinet door open. The shaft yawned out of sight, but the cords were still there, dangling in the darkness like belfry ropes. The gears and pulleys that the cords laced through drank oil thirstily, until they were slick with it. He pulled cautiously on the old rope. The metal wheels moved slowly, sleepily. But the more rope passed through them, the better they worked, until the rope sang through their grasp. He looked down, and his heart skipped a beat. There was a dumbwaiter still attached, just as Lauren had said. It jerked out of the darkness in a fog of dust. It wobbled a little, but the whole affair seemed sturdy enough.

He had to recite a whole poem before he had the nerve to get into the dark box with his flashlight.

He knew what Daddy would say, if he could see

him. He would shake his head and wonder aloud if his son had good sense.

The rope might be rotten down below. Jason could fall in this old thing and die. Then a black feeling came over him. It didn't matter what happened. Nothing could be as bad as the way he felt now.

He took a deep breath and began lowering himself. The pulley occasionally made cricket noises, and the rope that had already passed through it disappeared, black with oil, into the slot on the floor. But anyone hearing it would only think it was one of the common noises of the old house. He passed between floors slowly.

Then a pale light appeared at his feet; it grew as the box edged downwards. And he could hear the radio. He had reached the bottom of the shaft. The basement.

All he could do that first time was sit in the blackness and listen. He was too afraid to pry the door open, even a crack. Sometimes he could hear Lauren hum, and sometimes she would sigh hugely and sort of mutter to herself. It made Jason crazy to see what she was doing, but there was no way to accomplish that.

Later that night he watched her at supper, but she looked no different. *It* had not told her what he was up to. Or maybe the Bear had not seen him.

He was free to travel in the dumbwaiter, then.

That night he went down again and pried the dumbwaiter door open with a screwdriver. A bookshelf was in front of it, but he could see most of the basement through the crack. There was only a barren room in his flashlight beam, with a table loaded with paints and bottles and brushes. A painting was on an easel, but covered. His disappointment ached. Still he didn't know what she was pretending to paint.

From then on, he had something to do after school. He would make a racket coming home, and then sneak into his secret elevator and ride down to watch Lauren paint. Watching her gave him a feeling of power. He could descend right into the heart of her lair, and the Bear didn't know.

His heart sank when, on the third day, her easel was turned at an angle that allowed him to see. She only painted silly things. It was the kind of art they always hung over sofas at Sears. Not real art. Not the kind of creation Jason and Tilda had been reaching for. A feeling of superiority swelled inside him.

She sat on a stool, back to him, and hunched broodingly over the canvases. There was a farm scene first, with a silo and chickens in the yard.

After that she painted an autumn landscape, with hunting dogs bounding through. Irish setters. Later, she painted horses at a river. All in tiny, darting strokes of color so that a tree was just a swarm of little green marks. Not the way you really saw things at all. Her paintings were dumb.

And he could tell that she didn't like them either. Sometimes, after working for an hour on something, she would suddenly get up and stalk to the back of the room and look at it, chin in hand. She stood only a few feet from where he watched. Then her mouth would shrink with anger, or her shoulders would sag, and she would paint out what she had done. Sometimes, she just looked at the pictures until Jason was forced to go back upstairs out of boredom.

But still he went down every day. It made him feel better. After the misery of school, Jason could descend in the dumbwaiter and search for the answer to a more solvable riddle. For there was something familiar about Lauren now; something familiar and odd and both fascinating and sinister at the same time. She had noticed him, upstairs, looking at her. She was getting suspicious. And that keened the edge of his curiosity.

He came to understand slowly, like the developing of a picture in a tray of chemicals. Husky, gruff down here in her den, she walked the way *it* walked, rollingly. And those round shoulders and those surly glances. It chilled him to the heart.

Lauren was the image of the Bear.

11

JASON'S heart stopped in the night, and he awoke.

A cry that did not seem his own still echoed in his room. The dream had been savage and relentless. He had been in the math room. But the desks were higher than his head, and something in the room was after him, scrabbling among the metal legs of the desks. He had run from aisle to aisle, hiding. Sometimes he could glimpse a burning eye, or a claw, between the rows. He found brutally chewed pencils and ravaged books left for him, along with shredded photographs. On the pieces of photo were fragments of faces he could recognize.

The eye of Cleve's cousin Tilda, part of his mother's hair. Over all, there was the choking smell of turpentine. And then he had turned a corner and come face to face with the monster. It seemed his heart stopped then.

Now he was alone and totally awake. Trembling, he got out of bed and went into the hall. The house was still. Moonlight invaded the windows and carved frosted squares on the floor. Outside, the world looked crisp and abandoned. The church steeple rose like a silver spear.

He had drifted away from Cleve, but he hadn't been able to bear giving up the midnight walks altogether. Sometimes the night would call him, and he would have to go. It was calling him now. He would walk, and it would calm him.

He dressed in two layers of clothes against the cold and went out the tower window the way he had done when he and Cleve were prowling. He left the window open so he could return that way, but only a sliver so the draft wouldn't wake anyone.

As soon as he was away from the Castle, his feet found the proper pace. Walking gave his thoughts a beat to travel on. That way he was free of the Bear's deadly gravity, which pulled his mind into orbit around certain thoughts and kept them there. Now he could keep ahead of the feeling that the

Bear brought, the leaden doubt, the cold fear. The depression.

He felt freer when he walked.

The November cold was already numbing his face and burning at his ears, but he didn't mind. In a way, he liked it. It was a clean pain, and there was a reason for it. And when he got back to the Castle he would burrow under the sheets and try to remember how cold he had been.

His feet echoed down Walnut Street and Willowbranch, near the zoo. There were no crickets now, and most of the dogs were huddled inside against the cold. The world seemed deserted, and he seemed the last creature alive on the frozen, sunless planet.

Perhaps not.

He heard a sound as he turned down an alley off Lee Street. He turned, but only noticed the rustling of a bush against a high brick wall. He had startled a bird or something. Maybe a rat. He continued up the alley and came out on Stonewall Street. It was then that he caught a glimpse of something· out of the corner of his eye, behind. He whirled this time, but missed it. Had he really seen a puff of steam rising from behind the wall, as though some tall person were breathing heavily?

Or some tall thing.

He walked faster, and his mind was not as free as before. He turned around at the next corner, swiftly. There! A shadow moved against the side of a house as though something following him were ducking between the buildings to avoid being seen.

A chill much deeper than November lanced through Jason, and he stood paralyzed, watching. The shadow shimmered. It swayed back and forth in the electric streetlight.

He knew what moved that way, rocking from paw to paw as it sniffed the freezing breeze for scent of its prey. Clever, clever beast to mimic the way a bush moves in the winter wind. No one would have known it was the Bear but Jason.

Jason stepped quickly down the street, his knees stiff from the cold and the bulk of his double pants. When he turned the first corner, he broke into a run that became a wild dash. He cut between two houses and squeezed through a prickly hedge into a dark alley. It ran through three city blocks, away from the light. He wouldn't be obvious there, and he could take any exit he wanted.

He ran along the dirt path, along the rows of garbage cans, heading back toward Stonewall Street. He would try to confuse what followed him by doubling back. The hedge ended, and streetlamp light suddenly washed over him so that he had to crouch as he ran. Beyond was a vacant lot thick with withered sage that could hide him well enough until he reached the street. Then he could only dash across the bright, naked road into the next dark corridor.

He had seen the puff of breath here. But now he was heading the other way, and the wall was on his left. Halfway down the alley his foot hit a can. Like thunder it rattled ahead of him, announcing him to the world.

Panic shoved him into a scrambling run, and he nearly fell. But toward the end of the alley he forced himself to slow. He turned and looked through the tunnel of darkness, the streets like pale dashes cutting the alley. The silhouette he feared was not there.

He had fooled it. He grinned, though it hurt his frozen face.

Then he heard the snuffling on the other side of the wall. It was low, near the ground, a searching, sandpaper noise. It could have been the sound of bare bushes rasped against the wall by the wind. But this was different, purposeful, semi-intelligent. It had heard the can. He knew it had. And then he remembered with a horrible rush that this was not an ordinary bear. It was a spirit-bear, a bear that could jump through time and space. It had arrived ahead of him, and it was coming around the wall for him.

Jason ran back the way he had come, blindly, and when he came to the first street he turned and ran down it. He didn't care about the sound of his running. He didn't care if he woke up the whole neighborhood. Yes, that's it! If they came out, the Bear would go away!

But no one woke up, though Jason raced through their streets like the clatter of an army. No lights went on.

The cold air tore in and out of his lungs. It felt like jagged ice, and his breaths were gasps. He didn't look around, couldn't slow enough to look because he knew the thing was just a shuffle and a lunge behind him, grinning with a thousand cold teeth.

He turned down a dead-end street by mistake and had to tear through a weed-filled lot to get out. The brush pulled at him and sucked at his legs, but he broke through into an unknown street before he fell. Pain raked across his face. Cold pain, from bramble-claws. He tore his way up from the stones and stumbled on, then staggered onto a smooth lawn and tripped hard. His head thudded against a door.

The trees behind him whipped wildly with sudden wind, or perhaps the passage of a great animal, for his face was too numb to feel the wind. He reached up and found a doorknob, twisted it, and fell headlong into a room. He couldn't go on.

But, miraculously, the wind whistled, and before he could look up, the door slammed behind him. He was inside, and safe. The wind whirled, muffled by walls, and various trees whispered dryly against eaves. He knew the Bear was masked by those noises as it snuffled in frustration outside.

Jason stood up, wincing at the pain in his knees. Gradually his breathing slowed as he realized where he was. He groped down an aisle until moonlight from a high window fell across him. It was not silver against his jacket as it should have been. It was purple and crimson and royal blue, with a spider's web of lines binding them. He looked through the stained glass at the glow of the moon. It shone through Jesus' robe, and to Jason the light seemed warm.

The wind died, and silence replaced it. The Bear was gone, he somehow knew. Somehow, he had beaten it. The side door of the church had not been left unlocked by chance. He had found sanctuary.

He sat on the second pew and rested his head against the first. The wind came up again, found its angry way inside the church steeple and rustled against the belfry ropes. It died as suddenly, but in the silence the bells faintly hummed to mark its passage. And it seemed the bells had driven it away. He felt as if he had come home. He had not understood how bad he had felt recently, until that moment. It was as if he had been walking in a suit of lead, and now it was gone.

He found a pledge card in a rack on the back of the pew and a pencil. By the colored moonlight he wrote the word *home*. Then, word by word and line by line a poem followed as though dictated by another voice.

This was, he realized, the Final Sanctuary, the good one taken by Mother and Tilda, as they lay in their boxes and the organ music swelled around them. The Bear could not follow into this kingdom. Here was a refuge, if he could escape no other way.

He wrote it all in the poem, and then folded it into his pocket. Now that he knew there was a way out, he was not afraid to open the door and take the long, cold journey back to the Castle.

12

AFTER that night, Jason found that the only safe place was near Lauren. Somehow, if he clung close to the Castle, the Bear did not appear. It was as if it had driven him into her grasp and was prowling about only to drive him back into the Castle if he tried to escape.

The winter grew grayer and colder. The hearts of the trees froze. And, for Jason, the sun became a legend he had heard of as a child. The depression tightened around him.

Every day after school, he took the dumbwaiter down to the basement studio and stared into the dagger of light that the door's crack let in. And there she sat, making her stupid, common pictures. All her turpentine and her varnish and her fancy oils seemed able to paint were farm scenes and autumn fields. Jason knew that his father had had no luck in getting the little art galleries in the region to take the paintings. He could only get them hung in banks and a few restaurants. Jason had heard them talking about it in quiet tones one night. It was no wonder. The paintings were stupid.

Yet, though he hated her pictures, he could not stop his visits, and eventually he began to suspect she knew he was there. She started talking to the paintings, the hunting dogs and the cows in them. She told them her feelings. But Jason felt as if he were the real target of her words. She apologized to the canvases for not being able to paint them better. She told them that she was afraid she couldn't paint well. Then, for long periods she only stared at them.

Jason knew she was really mocking him. She pretended that her feelings were like his: that she wanted to do better but couldn't. She was stealing Tilda's moods, now that her Bear couldn't hurt Tilda anymore. It was like grave-robbing. And Lauren wore the captured feelings to make Jason think she was like him. But she was laughing at him all the time. She was not like him.

That's why he started writing the poems.

He wrote them in the dumbwaiter when he was full of anger. Anger that she was making fun of the way the Bear made him feel. They rattled out of his fingertips onto the paper by themselves, one a day for five days. They were about her paintings, or sometimes about Lauren herself.

He didn't know what to do with them, at first. They didn't belong with his other poems. They were about *her*. They would contaminate the others. He kept them in the dumbwaiter until there were too many.

Then he had an idea. It was dangerous, but one day somehow he found the guts to do it. When she was gone, he slipped out and put a poem by her painting. It had the desired effect. Lauren tore the poem up, cursing, after she read it. Then she went looking for him, but he was not upstairs. When she got back to the basement, she cried. That was when he knew it was worth the risk.

He was braced for the worst. But Lauren never said anything about the poems, even when one appeared almost every day. She often gave him a funny look, but it was as if they shared a secret between them. And that Jason could not understand. He knew it was crazy, risky, to do what he had done. And he had expected some result. Maybe he had thought she would show them to Daddy, and there would be a confrontation. Then at least he could get everything off his chest. He could tell Daddy how evil she was.

In a way her silence scared him even more than if she had told. She was up to something, and there was no way he could know what that was. Yet he could not resist writing new poems. That way, at least he was fighting.

She began locking the basement door behind her. The poems appeared anyway. Sometimes he thought she was as afraid as he was. It was clear she did not know he could use the dumbwaiter; the Bear had not told her that.

He wrote a new poem very carefully, one letter at a time in the sliver of light, the paper held against the back of the dumbwaiter. It was about the latest farm painting. It told her how the silo looked like a sausage, and how the chickens looked giant compared to the size of the tractor. He wrote the poem as if the painting were a nightmare he was having. He wrote that he'd had the same dream before, only with different farmhouses and fields, and how awful it was to dream the same thing over and over.

And he wrote more.

His blood galloping, he wrote about the Bear. He told her how she looked like the familiar, shuffling and pawing about the basement, with one fist in a jar of paint instead of honey. He mocked them both. Both so clever, and neither one knew where he was hiding.

The poem was funny. He almost laughed in the darkness. Then, he waited. Finally, Lauren pushed away her easel and put her palette down. She stretched.

"Chick, chick, chick," she muttered to herself. "Are you real chickens? Would you convince anyone? Or are you just gobs of brown paint? With a few little white touches?"

She was doing it again, and it made Jason glad he had written the new poem.

"Well, maybe you'll look like chickens when I come back," she said, and shuffled out the door. She closed it behind her and locked it.

That was Jason's signal to action. He worked immediately against the dumbwaiter door, jarring it open against the bookshelf that held it shut. If he did it carefully, he did not disturb the books, just simply moved the case out enough for him to squeeze through the door. Then he raced to her easel. There was a pushpin stuck in it that she used to pin up pictures of things she was painting. He used it to hang his poem. Then he slid back into the dumbwaiter. Using a coat hanger, he jerked the bookcase back in front of the dumbwaiter door and waited in quiet excitement.

Soon, the doorknob rattled. She was back from seeing to supper, or going to the bathroom, or whatever. She froze when she saw the paper pinned to the easel. Angrily, she ripped it off and threw it to the floor, then looked wildly around for someplace she had missed, someplace he could have been getting in. Her wide eyes raked around the room, and he drew back from the crack when she looked his way. Desperately, she climbed on her chair and searched behind the ventilation ducts with a broomstick. When she climbed down, her arms were limp and she wore a defeated expression. She sat like a bundle in her chair.

Jason's heart soared. He was paying her back for all his hours of pain under the Bear. For the math. For the dishes.

Lauren mumbled again. "How does he get in?" she whispered to herself. And then she noticed the poem and picked it up. She read it for a long time without changing expression. And she did not tear it up. She looked at the painting.

"He's right, my chickens." She spoke to the picture again. "The little devil's right. I *am* having the same dream, and it's a bad one. I don't blame people for not buying this stuff. Neither would I."

After a long pause, she said, "But, I want to be so *good*. I used to think, 'If only I had the time. If only I didn't have to work all day at this stupid job, I could concentrate on my painting. It would get better and better, the more I did.' Now, I find out it's so hard, so hard to believe in what I do."

Jason stopped grinning. He wanted to rip the dumbwaiter door open. She was making fun of him again. She was pretending to have the same kind of feelings he had. She, who was the Bear, pretended it was after her, too. He was glad he had told her about the Bear, now.

"Maybe he's right about that, too," she said in a whisper he had to strain to hear. "Maybe that's why I can't paint. I'm a bear." With a limp hand she threw her paintbrush at the canvas. It bounced off, leaving a brown blob against the silo in the farmyard.

"I'm a great, lumbering bear!" she shouted at the picture. "I wallow around in paint!" She threw a tube of oils at the painting and missed. "I want to paint like a human, I want to make the things in my mind come to life, but I end up making stupid bear-prints."

Then she made a sound that raised the hair behind Jason's ears and made him back away further from the sliver of light.

It was a bear-growl. She stood and waddled toward the painting, imitating an angry bear, waving her arms.

"Owwwwrrrrooorrrrrrroooorrr."

Jason went cold inside. He huddled closer to the back wall of the dumbwaiter. Here was proof of the Bear, if he ever needed it. He wished Cleve could see. The sight of Lauren hunched over with her claws held out terrified him. He had seen it before, chasing him through moonlit streets.

Lauren turned her head up and laughed, then collapsed back into her chair. But there was something close to pain on her face.

"Would that scare some life into you, chickens, if I were a big bear like the kid says? Maybe that's what I should do. Maybe I should try to be a bear."

She said something else then, Jason was sure of it, in a low voice. Her head was down, her hair hiding her face. She slowly turned her face up and spoke louder, as if she were addressing the Castle at large.

"Would that please you, my secret poet? If I were a bear?" Her eyes glistened as she spoke toward Jason's room.

In the dumbwaiter, Jason was suddenly sure she knew exactly where he was. This was a performance. For him. She had lured him down here and tricked him into giving away his deepest secret. She had made him show his poetry. He was naked to her, and horribly revealed in the dark.

He went through the motions of being a student the next day. But the hours at school were a drab shell to him. The only thing that mattered was getting back to the shelter of the Castle. He had to climb into the coffin of the dumbwaiter before he could return to life.

What was she doing, he wondered during science and deadly math. What was she doing now that he had given himself away? As he ate, he felt something developing, something growing and evolving back in the dungeons of his new home. Lauren had come to see him in his room last night, again. He had been as cold as ever, but she had insisted on talking to him. She had tortured him with words, pretending to be interested in him.

And he knew showing his poems had changed something about Lauren, and the Bear. He had made a mistake.

The feeling grew more intense when he came to the hill of the Castle. When he got to the top of the tower, his blood was pounding in his ears. Only when he climbed into the box beside his room did he begin to feel calm returning. But as he drew the rope through its circuit and descended, the calm began turning into an odd new feeling. It made his breath come slower and his grip on the cord turn to iron. Then he came to the basement.

She was painting. Not sitting in the chair, but standing, leaning into the canvas, intent. And the easel was turned at an angle too sharp for him to see the picture. His throat tightened more. All day waiting, and he still could not see what she was doing, how his stolen secret had changed her ability.

Then he saw the other painting behind her, against the wall. It was the barnyard picture, the one with the chickens.

She was painting something new.

He understood.

It was his soul she was painting. That had been her plan all along, and he had fallen into it perfectly. She had taken the power from his poetry and made it her own. She had cleverly, cleverly, let him think she didn't know where he was, let him think the poems were hurting her. When really, the poems were feeding her power. His magic had been sucked from him in the night, as a vampire might take blood.

Her body tried to stop painting several times. She put her palette down twice, but noticed something on the canvas each time before managing to leave and returned to make another daub of color on it. That lasted half an hour. Then, finally, she put things down and went out.

Jason opened the dumbwaiter door before she had turned the key in its lock. He ran to the painting. And yet he saw what was on the easel too soon.

He should have known.

The Bear reared, a great dark shape filling the canvas. Its teeth were bared. The sky behind it was a red whirlpool, centering on its sparkling, shimmering eye. Only one eye—its head was turned. It was laughing, sneering horribly as it danced out its heavy triumph. It laughed at Jason.

Now he knew what the calmness had been turning into. He was numb all over.

His poems were pinned to the easel for her to look at instead of pictures. Some of the ones she had torn up were pieced and taped together. They were like pale, dead leaves crucified against a dead tree.

Everything, everything was lost.

13

THE NEXT time he went down in the dumb-waiter, the bear painting was gone.

There was another in its place. This one had been painted fast and scratchy, and it was bigger than the first. The canvas exploded with the beast, all red and blue-black. And Lauren was bent close to its surface, her brush darting, poking, stabbing. Then she would step away for just a second and return.

Inside his cage, Jason felt a numbness crawl into his arms and legs. It came from inside him, from the back of his neck and the pit of his stomach.

And it was worse, much worse, than fear. Each brush stroke Lauren made stole some color from his insides and wiped it across cheap canvas. And it was all his fault, all his mistake. He had given her that power.

And now the next move was up to Lauren.

He expected it, and he was not surprised when she came to his room to say good night. He was tired and drained, so he let her come in and sit on the edge of his bed without even glowering at her.

Her eyes as she came in were turned away. And even when she spoke, she did not meet his gaze. That puzzled him. He had thought she was coming to gloat. But she just talked about daily things in her mildest voice, without facing him.

As she left, she bent down, and for a moment of terror he thought she was going to kiss him. But he went all rigid and flinched away, and she left the room without coming closer.

The next night she appeared again, and the next night. It was as if she were paying him back for his daily visits to her studio. And each time she talked—casually, but carefully—taking longer to say good night each time. Jason was not fooled. He could feel the prying in her questions about school, and especially about how he was doing in math.

She was after something. She was not finished with him yet.

Daily the numbness increased. It spread like a slow flood. His skin still touched things, but the feeling was not a live one. He no longer liked moving about a lot; he sat still for long periods. And his thoughts came very slowly through the layers of confusion.

Mrs. Quarterman passed out exam papers for math. But he could not smell the pungent purple ink on them. And the problems that crawled all over the pages were like nothing he had ever seen. He tried to do them. It took fifteen minutes for him to do the first problem, and then he had erased through the paper on almost every line. The answer was wrong—he knew it.

"Jason?" he heard the voice call distantly.

He looked up. It was Mrs. Quarterman leaning close, with a strange look on her pinched face.

"What's the matter, boy? Aren't you even going to try?" For the first time she was not yelling at him. She whispered. He could feel her breath.

He thought of a thousand things to say, but none of them had the power to make his tongue move, so at last he just looked down and shook his head. Shame was only a faint burning on the edge of his ears.

"Well, please try. Remember what we talked about doing with the positive and negative numbers . . . the mirror trick."

Then she was gone. The bell rang later, but he had not moved. His test was empty, and he turned it in without caring.

A gray sky followed him to the Castle.

When Lauren sat on the edge of the bed that night, she still smelled of turpentine. There was a red stain over most of her thumb. And she looked at him, right into his eyes. Somehow, he managed enough hatred to stare back.

"You didn't say much tonight at supper," she said softly.

He shrugged.

"You didn't even laugh at Daddy's joke. About the Baptist minister who went to heaven and ran into the Methodist." She giggled, and her heavy shoulders shook.

"It wasn't funny," he said. "I don't believe in heaven."

That made her smile turn odd shapes. She looked away and then slowly returned her gaze to him. "I'll tell you something. I'm not sure I do either. I know there's a hell, though." She sighed, then.

I'll bet you do, he wanted to say.

"Did you hear your daddy say he had to go up to Atlanta tomorrow? Up to the farm show. He'll be gone for a few days. He wanted me to tell you that he's worried about you, though. He wanted to

tell you, but . . . you know how he is. He doesn't
know how to talk to you very well."

You mean you won't let him.

"He got a call from Mrs. Quarterman today."

Jason's lip twitched and curled.

"We're both worried about you." She looked
away slowly and then back to him. "Can you tell
me what's going on?"

He shrugged again. "Nothing. I just can't do
math. I'm not smart in math."

"You could have filled out . . . it's just not
good not to *try* on something like that. Mrs. Quarterman says she wants you to take it over, when
you feel like it."

"I'll never feel like it."

She nodded, to his surprise. "It must seem that
way. We've all noticed how you've changed. We
all want you to feel better. You have to understand
that you will feel better."

We. You and the Bear.

"You've had a rough year. The move was hard
on you, I know. And I wasn't much help, I bet,
with all the law I laid down. Please understand how
nervous I was about doing things right, about being
your . . ."

She didn't say it, and he was glad. *Mother.*

"I know you knew Cleve's cousin. Your daddy

and I feel that what happened with her might be bothering you, and we wanted you to know . . ."

The look in his eyes stopped her. *No. You can't touch Tilda. You can't talk about her.* Suddenly, the numbness was broken by a savage fear that Lauren was prying too close.

"That doesn't have anything to do with it," he snapped.

For a long moment she didn't say anything. "Do you want to talk to your daddy about anything?"

"No."

"Do you want to talk to Brother Ivey, from the Church . . ."

"NO!" Hissed.

Her shoulders slowly sagged, and she turned away. He could not tell whether in anger or defeat, and he did not care.

"Good night," she said. The bed creaked when she got up. But at the door she stopped and turned her head slightly back toward him.

"I know how you feel, Jason."

Yes. You sent the feeling.

"I know because I've felt that way, too. A lot, until recently. Even when I was a little girl."

Lies. Mockery. Cruelty.

"It'll get better. You just wait. We're a lot alike, in some ways. We're both creative. We make reality out of things we imagine. That's why it's so difficult to get together."

No. No. No. I could never be like you.

"Good night," he said coldly.

And the darkness came again, a place in which hidden dreams danced and spun. The Bear did not even appear, though the slippery shapes of Jason's dreams smelled of the creature. The Bear was waiting for something, to deliver the final blow. It was gathering strength. He knew it.

And when he knew that, the last surge of anger came to him. He had to fight his way out of this pit. He had to fight the Bear.

He tried. He sweated through school, trying to find some will to understand. He went back over his old math notes, and his hands were always white with struggle. Mrs. Quarterman talked to him and made a new date for his test.

But, once in the Castle, the numbness returned. It rushed back and swept over him, and he stopped for a long time between floors in the dumbwaiter. It was darker than night there, quieter than the center of the earth. He wanted to stay there, between things, forever.

There were more bears in the studio. The radio played triumphant music, and the paintings were stacked. Daddy had taken some of them away, off to galleries and banks. Lauren hummed to herself as she painted.

And Jason did not stay. He could not stand to watch her energy and her joy, which had been stolen from him. He went back upstairs.

Supper came and went quickly, like a light passed in a tunnel. The others talked about things, and Jason moved most of his food to the edges of his plate to make it seem he had eaten.

Lauren came to his room again. The light was off, but he could hear her opening the door.

"Jason? Are you asleep already?"

He stirred in bed, and she turned on the light. He hid his eyes with one hand.

"Why are you in bed? It's awful early." As she sat on the bed, she put a hand out to feel his forehead for fever, and she almost touched him.

"I'm tired," he said.

"You are? I'd forgotten kids could get tired, too."

"Good night."

"Not yet," she said. "I need to tell you something first. I've made a decision."

His stomach tightened. He looked at her eyes, which were looking at the floor. Something was in them, a spark. Her power was increasing.

"What?" he said woodenly.

"I've decided it's time for me to go back to work. Mr. Abernathy spoke to me the other day and told me how much they miss me, and they'd like to have me back."

Jason's mind tumbled. "But—what about your painting? You just quit work!"

She smiled. "I know. Seems a little silly, doesn't it? But there it is."

"But, *why?*"

"I don't know. I guess, in a way, I feel that I've proved something to myself. Maybe to the world. I've always wanted to be a working artist. Now I can say I have been."

"But, you hated working for them."

"Not really. I've found out in the time I've been working at home that I miss all the people. It can be pretty tough being alone with yourself all day. Too much time to think. Anyway, I'll still have time to paint, on weekends and at night. It'll be easier, now that I know how to paint."

He didn't say anything. He didn't know what to think or say.

She paused, then looked directly at him. "You know I haven't been painting the same old things lately."

He didn't move.

"There's something new in my paintings. I always thought you had to paint what you knew. Now I've been taught a different way to paint—that if you paint with your heart, the subject doesn't have to be familiar. It just has to be what's inside you.

"I just wanted to tell you . . . thanks. You know what I'm talking about. You know why I'm painting differently. Thank you."

Then she was gone.

The next day was his math make-up test. Mrs. Quarterman walked him down to the library and handed the papers to him and told him to take as long as he wanted. She left, and there was only he and the librarian, who was out of sight. The room was filled with the odor of old books and new test papers.

It was a different test, but the problems were the same sort. And as soon as he put his pencil to the paper, his strength began leaving him. He really wanted to try, this time. But he couldn't keep his mind working. He began sweating; it ran down his neck like ice water. The rules he had memorized wouldn't work, or suddenly the words didn't mean what he thought they did. It was all as useless as before.

He was cold, inside and out. He turned the test in half done and all wrong. Mrs. Quarterman did not say anything to him, but there was anger, and something else, in her eyes. Disgust, maybe.

The rest of the day fluttered by like a memory; and then the Castle loomed for him, hollow and cold. Empty. He was the ghost that haunted it until the Foreign Princesses came to fill its halls with laughing life.

14

LAUREN came home from her first day back at work, and then soon after Daddy was there too, back from his trip. He was flushed and grinning and seemed excited and happy to be home. He hugged Lauren over and over. Jason saw it from the top of the stairs, where he stood hidden in the shadows. He wondered if Daddy had ever hugged his mother like that.

After supper, Jason found out why Daddy grinned so much. It was another after-dinner speech, and he was so built up he was sweating.

"Ladies and gentlemen of the Barnett clan," he said. "I have the great pleasure to make two important announcements tonight. First . . . you all know Lauren here has gone back to work for Abernathy. Well, today she found out she's not just a bookkeeper any more. She's Head Bookkeeper. That's a bigger job, and she's got a raise!"

Daddy held up his long bony hands to stop the Princesses' shrill acclaim. For a moment his eyes touched on Jason, but not long. "Wait . . . wait. That's just the warm-up!"

Even Lauren was now looking at Daddy expectantly. She had not heard this news either. There was tension in her.

"I came through Stewartville today, on my way home. And I stopped by the Wainwright Gallery. I left some of Lauren's pictures with them last week, and I wanted to check up."

There was silence around the table as Daddy fished in his shirt pocket. Then he slowly withdrew a folded slip of paper. He handed it to Lauren.

"Mrs. Barnett, I'm proud to bring you the check for your first commercial sale. You're an artist!"

There was more shouting and jubilee, and through it Jason sat still as a rock. But he could still hear, and through the noise he heard Lauren ask which picture had sold, and he heard the answer.

No one noticed him leave the table and make his way up to his room.

It was the Bear, the first painting of the Bear that had sold.

He sat at his desk for a long time, with paper and pen, trying to make words come. He had felt patterns of words, dimly, somewhere inside him. But they had vanished. He wanted to write it down, about the numbness that was replacing feeling. But he couldn't.

Lauren had taken it. His ability. She had used the Bear to trick him into giving away his creativity.

There was very little left to do.

He thought of Tilda, as he lay waiting for Lauren's visit. And he thought of his mother. And Pablo, the collie. Already he felt the solution he had come to taking away his fear. He drifted into sleep.

He was awakened when he felt the bed jar. It was Lauren, settling into her perch on the edge. She looked at him directly this time, smiling. He had never noticed how her face crinkled in places when she did that. Maybe she had never smiled that way before.

Smile. It's all right. You can't touch me now.

"You fell asleep with the light on, fella."

He did not answer, nor make a move.

"Are you all right? You went upstairs awful early tonight."

"I was through."

She looked at him for a long moment, as if she were surprised he was speaking to her. As if she noticed something in his tone.

"I missed hearing you bumping around upstairs today. I hope you weren't too lonely here by yourself."

"I'm never alone in this house," he said slowly, carefully. There was no longer any need to hide things. "Congratulations."

"Congratulations?"

"On the painting."

Her smile broadened. "Thank you. That means a lot, coming from you. You know why that particular picture sold, don't you?"

He knew.

"That was the breakthrough painting. That's the one that taught me to stop repeating myself, to stop worrying about what people might think of my paintings. That's the first one that had life in it."

My life.

"Thank you," she said softly.

His lips sneered, without his control. "Why thank me?"

She blinked. "Because you showed me how to paint. You showed me how to make my brush feel. Anger, at first. Your . . . poems showed me that. But then . . . I don't know. There was so much

life and rhythm in those little notes. I stopped wondering how you got them down there. Your poems
taught me. That's why the painting sold. It was the
first one with poetry in it."

And hate.

"And love," she said. "A wild love of living. A
savage one. And it gave me the strength to tell you
this."

Lauren's hand hovered and dropped onto his
chest. Its ugly warmth burrowed toward him
through the blanket. He flinched.

"I've come to feel very deeply about you, Jason.
Please, please listen. We're citizens of a similar
kingdom. But it's a country of the blind, so we
didn't recognize each other. But now I know. We
belong together.

"I love you," she said.

His face tensed into a mask, with a line for lips.
"That's too bad, because I hate you."

Her smile faded, then dropped off, and her hand
twitched. She stared at him.

"I hate you because you're fat and ugly, and you
took Daddy. I know you're lying—all you want is
to torture me and drain me away in the night so
you can fill your paintings with my stuff. You've
dried up my poems. And now you want the rest of
me. No! You can't have me!"

He hissed the last, and her hand shot back as though from a serpent. Her face twisted.

"You sent him! You sent the Bear! You didn't paint him! You're the stumbling thing that I wrote about!"

She was standing now, under the light. Her hands went to her face.

"But that's okay," he continued. "I'm going. You can't have any more of me. You won't have to go to the basement to paint anymore. You can have *my* room!"

He only heard the door close; he never saw her leave.

He turned off the light and waited a long time for Daddy's footsteps up the stairs. But they never came, and that made him smile grimly. She was keeping it all to herself. She knew he was serious. Maybe she was a little scared.

For he knew now he would foil the Bear. He knew all he had to do was take sanctuary.

Final Sanctuary.

15

DARKNESS pressed its face to the window, a soft and choking thing like black cotton all outside the Castle. But Tilton was spread out there, too, spilled pieces of some vast Monopoly game, square houses, night avenues splayed across the hills. And among the scattered buildings, sanctuary called to Jason from a mute steeple.

Silent lightning popped crisply faraway. Highlights, like frost, rippled over the sleeping town, marking his way.

His hands, cold on the cold of the window, pushed a way out into the night skillfully, without noise. As he had before, he slung a leg out, but he didn't think about the last time he had gone. This time was different. And besides, everything past was part of another life.

He could only think of the next step now. And it was hard, oh so hard to think. He sat on the window ledge forever, before he understood what to do next.

He fought his way down the tree. He was sweating, yet he was cold. The cold came from inside him, he realized finally. The air tonight was warm.

A storm was coming. Lightning flashed distantly within it. The town, the new place, the place they wanted to be his home, fluttered past and copied each flicker of lightning upon its walls.

He stumbled and found he was running and slowed. There were words in his mouth. A poem. The words came in time to his footsteps; saying them, he did not have to think of where to go, or why he was going.

> *Hear the tolling of the bells—*
> *Iron bells!*

Wind was beginning now. He said the words faster, and his feet answered with a quicker step. The trees whispered, danced, contorted along the streets. They would hide the rustling of the Bear, as before. The Bear was coming, wearing the storm like a cloak. The Bear was coming. The Bear was coming to stop him. Jason was trying to take the victim out of its reach. Out of *her* reach.

The Bear had to stop that!

> *For every sound that floats*
> *From the rust within their throats*
> *Is a groan.*

Each snap of lightning behind him sent a pale shadow ahead, running faster, trying to escape from him and pulling him on at the same time. He flew. And around him, the air growled with a presence.

> *Keeping time, time, time,*

It tried to make him stop and pushed thoughts he didn't want to think in his way.

> *In a sort of Runic rhyme,*

Then he was running up steps. The lightning spoke, and it uttered the name of a white finger, a bone, a tusk pointing up, away past the storm. Up, to show him where he had to go. A steeple.

The door rattled, locked; fury didn't budge it. But he knew the other door, the door Mother left unlocked for him that other time, and the echo of his footsteps chased him around back to it.

Of the bells, bells, bells—

Sanctuary. Darkness, an enclosed darkness without flashes or shadows, slammed behind him. The smell of organ music, Easter, Baptisms. The high windows. A storm-flicker through them dissolved lightning into the spectrum of a ghost.

He found more steps beneath him. But these were harder to climb, and spiral. And they went up and up, all enclosed, thick night, and the fever inside him made each step harder than the last. The Bear seemed to increase gravity; Jason's feet were stone, asleep, paralyzed. Sweat crawled in his face.

He heard a noise somewhere behind, in the church.

It was coming. It was inside. It had even found power to come here.

There was a window in the steeple, near the bells. He found himself there, looking down at the ropes when the lightning flashed. The ropes went down and down through the steeple, but he could not see their end. He knew it was far. He knew it would take a long time to reach their end. The rest of his life. Moments.

It seemed a dream. There was the Final Sanctuary, yawning. He could go where the Bear could not reach him. Yet his feet could not move.

There was a noise behind him, on the stairs. It spoke his name.

"Jason."

And, as if the word had been a blow, Jason lost his breath. A jolt went up his back, and then another wave came racing through him. It was triumph. Another step, and he was free.

"Don't go!" A whisper filled the steeple. But it was not the Bear that had spoken.

He half-turned, enough to see Lauren standing, white and huge, in the doorway. One foot was on the steeple platform.

"You can't have me," he said to his surprise. "I won't live like this any more. I'm going away where you can't send the Bear after me."

Darkness opened its arms for him. Invisible ropes pointed the way.

"Stay," she said, and there was an odd waver in her voice. "You're talking to the only person who knows the way you feel. I've been where you are. I've wanted to go that bad. To escape."

"*Lies!*" His shrillness shocked him, and he almost jumped.

She made a gasping noise. He felt her lunge in the dark.

"No! No! Don't come any closer!"

"Stay then. Just stay for a minute, and let me talk to you. I won't come any closer."

He didn't speak. He hesitated on the brink. Then lightning winked, and swimming in the inky air over the pit he saw a form. Only for a second, and the light was gone. But the wriggling, pawing image of the Bear was branded on his eyes.

"*It's here! You brought it!*"

She was behind him, and the Bear was in front. Pincers. Closing.

"No! No, Jason. I swear. I didn't bring anything. You . . . what did you see out there in the darkness?"

"Don't mock me! You brought the Bear. It's your Bear and your familiar, and now it's out there, and it won't let me go."

A pause. "My Bear? This thing that's tormenting you? Is that . . . Jason, is that why you wrote those poems? You weren't just making an image? It's a thing that's after you? I don't understand." Urgency in her voice.

"It's a Bear. It's your demon, and it lives off my

pain. It tricked me into giving you my poetry, s-so you could take its power. That's why your painting got better." He waved his arms in frustration. Why was she doing this?

"No, no," she said almost in a whimper. "I didn't send anything to hurt you. I just made a mess out of trying to be your mother. I know how you hurt. But I can help you find another way out of it. I know the way."

Lightning happened, thunderless. The animal squirmed in the half-light, beckoning, faceless. Fear took all the blood out of Jason's face and left him on a skillet of ice, shook him over the edge like a taunt.

"Wait . . . wait, Jason! Jason, what's the Bear doing? Can you see it?"

His eyes widened, the darkness pressed against them. "It wants me. It wants me to come to it."

"But I thought you wanted to escape it. You can't escape if you go to it. You can only go toward it if you step off."

"*No!*" She was trying to confuse him. "Stop it!"

"Don't go to it, Jason. That's what it wants. Talk to it. Make it answer you back. That's what I do with my paintings sometimes, and they talk to me. Make it tell you what it wants."

"Me! Me! It wants me!" He was crying, or ice picks were moving down his face.

"Bear!" Lauren bellowed, her voice raw as the night. "What do you want from Jason?"

A voice? A whispered, hissed reply twisted by the wind?

"What did it say? Did it say something?"

"It said: I want . . . I want his eyes . . ." Jason muttered.

"Ask it why it wants your eyes. Now, Jason!"

He asked it.

"Because you live in the daylight. Because you have a world."

When he repeated the answer to her, Lauren said, "What world is it from, Jason? It must live somewhere. How can it take your world?"

"Trade. Swap. Daylight here—night there. Come."

"It wants you to understand it, Jason!" she said frantically. "That's all. You don't have to die to do that."

"Release me!" Jason screamed. Something inside him was splitting in two.

"I speak for the land of the distant giants. Come."

He repeated the phrase in a tortured voice.

"Think, Jason. Distant giants. Who is a giant?

Who's gone away, and who's bigger than real living people? Ask it!"

He did. It said names. He screamed again and held his ears and danced on the edge of the belfry. It said *Mother*. And *Tilda*. It called to him from the sanctuary they had gone to. He screamed that he wouldn't listen, he wouldn't hear and he wouldn't ask it any more questions. He couldn't hear his own voice.

"Then make it show its face! Make it help you understand."

"No!"

"Whose face is it wearing? Jason, who is really the Bear?"

Ahead, in the river of midnight fog, the shape twisted in agony, but a pale wisp marked a face for it.

"It's you!" Jason howled. But he couldn't see. It was too dark. The shape came toward him, slowly, twisting.

"Who is the Bear, Jason?"

Suddenly, he didn't want to know any more. He only wanted to take the sanctuary he had come for. He wanted out. His muscles twitched as he bent to jump.

Lightning popped gently, outside. A face swam out of the night, clearly, filling everything.

"My face! Mine! I am the Bear!"

And he jumped. Or seemed to, as he remembered. It was a long, shattering leap. It was a leap that dissolved him and put his molecules back together at the same time. It was a leap from heart to heart. It was blood, and being born.

16

JASON'S eyes opened.

The night was angry. Clouds fought and wrestled, kicked and twisted, locked in a gray, swollen maelstrom high overhead. A high storm, a storm vast and so high that when lightning flickered in it there was no thunder. Only a lacework throbbing of light. Veins of fire. Internal glows.

A steeple stretched overhead and caught the glow of soundless lightning.

They were on the front steps of the church. He stirred and realized he was lying across Lauren's lap. His head spun, and he stopped moving. Why was he holding on to her like that? He was supposed to hate her.

He felt protected, suddenly. The Bear was gone. Vanished. There was no tug of it below his heart, in the muscles of his chest, where it had moved before.

Dreamily, he looked up and saw that Lauren had noticed him.

"It's gone," he said.

She only nodded. Then, after looking away, she said, "You let it go."

He slid away from her and found his own seat on the stone steps. How could *he* release the Bear?

"You saw through its disguise," she said quietly. Her voice was nearly hidden in the wind. "You made it tell you the truth, and that took all of its energy away. Like a balloon out of air, it flew away."

"But will it come back?" Her arm was warm beside him, and he leaned closer to it.

She sighed, a long one. "Oh, eventually, when you start forgetting again." She looked back at him. "When you forget that the pain you're feeling comes from inside you. It's yours. No bear brings it. When you forget that, a little energy that would have gone into understanding goes to the part of you that you call the Bear instead. It builds up and starts doing things to make more energy. It makes doubts and shows you bad things. The more energy you give it, the less you understand. It wants enough energy to make you see it."

He touched his face. A ripple went up his spine. "It wants my eyes."

"Yes." She nodded again. "But it's you. Remember that. What it really wants is to see with your eyes, as a part of you. When it comes back, it won't be quite as bad as this first time. I'll be there to help you. You're lucky. My first time lasted two years."

Jason sagged. "I can't face it again. I'm . . . weak."

Lightning lit her face and sparkled in her eyes, and anger shone there. For a minute Jason thought he had done the dishes wrong. "Don't ever say that. Don't ever let me hear you say you are not strong. You didn't jump. That's strong. You fought a monster for three months, and it didn't beat you. That's the best kind of strong."

"What's wrong with me, then? What made me do that?"

"Wrong? The same thing that's wrong with me. You want too much. You and I want to touch the stars. We create. You make poems, and I make pictures. Other people make other things. And we can never, never quite touch the sky. We can only just make our creations come close. And we disappoint ourselves because we can't reach. And we fall. It's twice as far down as it is climbing up. It hurts. But we have to keep trying for the stars, Jason, or it's no good. Keep trying."

He sank back into himself. Deep within a cloud, lightning erupted. "I want somebody to fix me," he said.

"There are no doctors for what we have, Jason. There are only people who want to help, and they call them doctors. But it's all inside you. No one goes in with a knife and cuts it out."

He trembled. "I've got a lot inside me, then. I've got kingdoms and castles and faceless things that guard them." He sat up. "The Bear came into my dreams before it showed up in the . . . house. Does that mean it was trying to wake me up, to make me understand it?"

She looked up, and her shoulders shook, and her teeth flashed with distant fire. "You're beginning! That's right. Pay attention to what you see in your dreams."

Then she looked down. "You know you're like me, don't you?"

He nodded. It did something to his insides, but he told the truth. "I—I think that's why I was so afraid of you. That's why the Bear looked like you. You paint, and I write. I—I hated it that you under-stood me better than she used to."

"Well. If you can admit that, you're on your way. You can't be so alone if you know you're not so unbearably unique."

They both chuckled at the word with the bear in it. She put her hand on his head and straightened his hair.

"You can come down from that mountaintop now and realize that you're on a plain, and there are other people on it. We have to help each other against the bears."

They were silent again. Thunder was beginning to echo now, sharper with the passing minutes. The wind bore moisture in it.

And Jason knew something. He knew that he had just buried his mother. She was gone now. And he let himself remember her. It was better to remember her than it had been to be with her. She had not understood him any more than Daddy had.

Lauren did understand. It made an acid taste on his tongue to know that. Lauren was his real mother now. He was like her. More like her than like his real mother.

"Come on," she said, hands on knees as she prepared to stand. "It's going to be raining. We have to get back before anybody notices we're gone."

The wind, cold now, whipped past them, and Jason leaned into her as they walked. He would not tell her now, that she was his mother. Perhaps some day he would. Maybe.

He made up a poem on the way back to the Castle and wrote it down later and kept it for a long time. He still has it. He carries it to remember, when a certain dark figure returns.

The poem ends:

Life is good, and mine,
And there is love,
Even in the Castle of the Bear.